The Doublooner

A Novel

by Weyman Jones

PUBLISH AMERICA

PublishAmerica

Baltimore

ISBN: 1-4137-0481-6
PUBLISHED BY PUBLISHAMERICA, LLLP
www.publishamerica.com
Baltimore

Printed in the United States of America

For Bob Jagoda — Prince of Limerick

CONTENTS

CHAPTER 1
A Rough Crowd

She walked along the edge of low tide, occasionally glancing toward the milky horizon, bare feet tracking straight lines along the saturated, quaking gray sand as if she were on a purposeful journey. She did not pick up shells or peer into tide pools. In the mid-morning heat she wore a floppy straw hat, sun glasses and two wisps of white swim suit under a teasing translucent white cover-up.

She did not glance at where I sat against the pine on the edge of the sand, recovering from a two mile dripping-humidity jog that was like running under water. I had been thinking that a career crisis at age fifty plus was like measles or mumps in adulthood: unseemly, and more dangerous than at the proper age. To change the subject in my mind, I imagined that she was watching for a returning seaman. The idea brought a smile. Not likely. Not in this day and age.

In the dense pine shade I thought I must be virtually invisible to her. But as she drew abreast she took off her glasses and looked directly at me. I started, feeling discovered, and then she was past, leaving an after-image of tilted, Oriental eyes, caramel skin and an edge of shiny black hair under the fluttering brim.

Watching her stride toward the point, where the bait fisherman paused to watch her pass, I decided that her face had come from Asia but her body from Africa by way of Europe. And I decided that in Key West, 24-hour party town full of pretty girls, a beautiful woman had just passed by.

No, not beautiful. Exotic. Erotic. Arresting. More than that. Stunning.

What was it she'd left behind? The beach was emptier now, the cry of the gulls more lonely. The rhythm of the surf more insistent. I tried to analyze the snapshot image of that lozenge face with a small straight nose and tilted dark eyes, those bobbing breasts and swelling hips. Was it a child's face in a woman's body? Voluptuous innocence? Was there something in that glance? An appeal? An invitation? Or was that purposeful stride making me more aware of my aimless hanging-on here in Key West, thinking about that ad in the *Citizen* to avoid returning to the furnished apartment in Norfolk that I called the Old Sailor's Home and look for a real job?

As she turned along the point toward Fort Zach, the bait fisherman cast a smooth back-hand motion, unfurling his leaded net into a twisting disk that landed with hardly a splash. Something in the lingering presence of the woman jumped a connection in my mind. Programmed by thirty years of military training to go from A to B to obvious, in her wake my mind now jumped from the bait fisherman to a fragment of a Tuscan frieze, a gladiator with his net and trident, that I'd seen while I was at the dé Licosa cooking school. At the time, I'd tried to visualize how such an awkward, entangling weapon as a net could be used in the arena. Now, watching the bait fisherman cast it as if tossing a frisbee, I almost understood.

I was still thinking about her, and about purpose, or lack of it, as I pedaled Harry's rusty old fat-tired bike in the gathering dusk from the beach back to the condo, which may be why I didn't notice the white Mercury parked in front of the moped rental shop on Duval. The cops must have been watching for a light in Harry's windows, because by the time I'd poured a glass of California Merlot and opened the sliders onto the roof terrace, they were knocking at the door.

"Mr. Malverne?" asked the shorter one, a solid little man of earth tones: gentle brown eyes, brown synthetic-tweed jacket over an off-white shirt and tie with ocher stripes. He flicked open a leather wallet to show me a police shield. The other one stood back.

"No, I'm his house guest. Is there a problem?"

"Is Mr. Malverne here?"

"No, he went back to New York. What's the problem, officer?"

"Could we come in for a minute?"

"I suppose – sure." I stood out of the way. The earth-tones cop went in but the other one, who I now noticed was taller and wearing a white open-collar knit shirt under a gray blazer, motioned me ahead of him.

Earth-tones said, taking the chair I offered, "I am detective Morales and this is my partner, detective Scully."

Scully flashed a smirk out of pointy, fox-face features that reminded me of the upperclassman who had made my plebe year miserable. As I sat in the facing chair, Scully drifted back into the kitchen, looking around.

"You said you're a house guest but your host has gone back to New York?" Morales said, in the Hispanic way of asking statements.

"Harry invited me down for some fishing. He left this morning – had to get back to the office – but the condo wasn't rented for the rest of the week and so he said I could stay on."

"You don't have an office to get back to, Mr....?"

"Bascomb. Burke Bascomb. And no, I'm retired." Behind him, in the entrance to the kitchen, the tall one jotted in a notebook.

Morales, still asking: "You look very young to be retired?"

"Military. Thirty years and out. Trying to decide what I want to do now. Why the questions, officer?"

Instead of an answer, another conversational question: "Do you know Mr. Armond? Paul Armond?"

I started to shake my head and then remembered: "Yes. Met him last night. Harry and I went to his party."

"Would you tell me about that party, Mr. Bascomb?"

"First, would you tell me what this is all about?"

The two cops exchanged a glance. Morales shifted slightly on the couch, but he answered in the same, off-hand way: "This morning Mr. Armond was found in his swimming pool."

"Found?" I repeated. "You mean…"

He nodded, watching my reaction. "I'm afraid so. We're talking to everyone who might help us understand what happened to him."

"I don't think I can be of much help. I just met the guy, talked to him a couple of minutes. Harry and I left early. Who found him?"

"Couple of–" another exchange of glances "–young men left over from the party. They say they came down around nine and saw him there."

"They *say* they did?" I prompted.

Morales leaned forward, elbows on knees. "We don't know how he got in the pool. Coroner is examining him now, but it wasn't an accident?" Turning that into a question seemed to ask if I understood.

I nodded and asked, "You think someone at the party…?"

He raised one hand in a not-so-fast gesture and shook his head. "We're talking to everybody who was there. Can you give us Mr. Malverne's New York number?"

"I've got it here somewhere," I said, fishing out my pocket calendar.

"Never mind," Scully said from the kitchen. "Its on the Rolodex by the phone."

I looked around and said, "Did you go through the closets too?" Scully just offered his upperclassman smirk.

Morales handed me a narrow notebook opened to a fresh page. "Could you write your name, your home address and number for me? And then we're going to want you to tell us everything you remember about the party?"

As I wrote I explained that Harry was an old Navy friend. When Morales asked how long I'd known him I said "since Nam."

"Tell me about that," he said, and so I explained that when Harry graduated from Yale, instead of taking one of the several available ways around Viet Nam he enlisted in the Navy, applied for flight school, washed out and became A-6 bombardier-navigator. He and I flew half a dozen tree-top missions, which makes for a lasting friendship, and we'd kept in touch after he he'd left the Navy to go into the real estate business with his father. They'd started coming down here – Harry and his father – for the tarpon run "when Sloppy Joe's was still on Greene Street" according to Harry, and so Harry was sufficiently established in Key West's conch society to be invited to Paul Armond's party.

"And at the party – you met a number of people?"

"Sure."

"Their names?"

I hesitated. "I don't remember. They were just – we just made party talk."

"You don't remember *any*one, Mr. Bascomb?"

"Well, sure. I remember Armond. Paul Armond. I told you that. And there were a couple of guys we had dinner with. A couple of couples, actually. But we weren't *with* them – just sat down at their table. I'm sorry, I was introduced, but I'm not good at names."

"You say, *we* sat down at their table. You and Mr. Malverne?"

"No. I had dinner with someone named Marge. Marge Landers."

Morales raised his eyebrows in an expression that seemed to say, "finally, we're getting somewhere," and made a note. "So you do remember Marge Landers. She must have made an impression." He smiled and denied the implications of that with a little gesture. "Which I can understand, of course."

"You know her?" I asked.

"Everyone knows Margaret's. Her restaurant." And then, still in the conversational tone: "How do you feel about homosexuals, Mr. Bascomb?"

Startled, I looked around. Scully was still projecting that slight upperclassman smirk from the entrance to the kitchen. After a moment, I said, "I don't have feelings about them, Detective. Why?"

"You must have encountered homosexuality in the Navy. How do you feel about it?"

"I feel that 'don't ask, don't tell' is a stupid non-policy that doesn't work."

"You'd like to go back to the policy that worked?"

"I didn't say that." I stood up to close this off. "Anyway, it's not my problem now."

Morales stood with me. "Do you have any other business here in Key West, Mr. Bascombe? Anything at all, other than fishing?"

I took a moment before answering, decided that more was safer than less and said, "Nothing specific, not yet. I'm interested – curious really – about an ad in the paper. Dive company that's looking for a cook."

Coming out of the kitchen entrance, Scully said, "Roger

Terrell?"

"Who's he?"

"Runs the Jolly Roger treasure barge. The guy who's advertising for a cook. You serious about that?"

"I don't know," I said. "Is he finding serious treasure?"

"He's serious about looking for it."

Morales offered a card. "We appreciate your cooperation. If you think of anything else – any other names of people you met, anything that happened–" he waved a "you know" gesture "– we'd appreciate a call?"

I showed them out and then stepped out onto the roof terrace where I could watch them get into their car and pull out of the strip mall, going back over last night in my mind to refresh my memory. When he mentioned the party and the woman he wanted me to meet, Harry had said that I could come as his date and, then, laughing at my reaction: "Won't bother them if you don't let it bother you. Half of them'll be gay, but a straight guy like you won't know which half. Point is, nobody gives a shit."

I rode his old bike – he said parking in Key West is worse than in Tokyo and so cars are strictly for tourists – and he walked with me down Truman and past St. Mary's Star of the Sea. On the way I asked, "So this woman you want me to meet – who'll she be coming with?"

"Last time I saw her she came alone. That's okay too."

"And you took her home?"

Harry waved a dismissive gesture. "Not me. My interest is pure greed. My old man couldn't ignore a business opportunity. So now I've inherited a piece of a tee shirt shop and a bed-and-breakfast along with a failing restaurant named Margaret's."

"The lady's name?"

"Sort of. You know Margarita's? Jimmy Buffet's place? Everybody does – that's the point. She positioned her restaurant against it. No glitz, out of the way where the tourists didn't find it, and named for the chef, not a drink. Actually, we all call her Marge, but she said a restaurant with that name would sound like a diner. She ran a super-chic place. You know, tofu creations and sashimi – exotica."

"And it's failing?"

"Used to net twenty per cent before taxes."

When I shook my head that I didn't have any context for that he explained: "Average is probably five per cent. Now, Margaret's is running a minus two or three per cent."

"Which means it's losing money?"

"My money."

"What happened?"

"Marge sold out. She and her husband had the controlling interest – Dad always wanted to be a silent partner down here."

"She has a husband?"

"Not any more. Got rid of him and the restaurant at the same time." We paused to give the right of way to a hen followed by half a dozen yellow fluff balls scratching in the litter around the curb. "Burke, nobody really knows what makes a restaurant go. Whatever it is, the new management doesn't have it. So now, instead of a piece of an income property, I have a cost center."

"And you think maybe I can get Marge back into the kitchen?"

Harry laughed. "I don't think King Kong could take Marge where she doesn't want to go. But you've been to that high-toned Italian cooking school – maybe you two can exchange recipes or something. Along the way, maybe you'll get a clue to what turns her on. Or off."

We stopped at a high gate of some kind of weathered wood that opened onto a narrow lane through specimen trees hanging with orchids and air plants. We left the bike on a casual heap of others and walked toward a throb of steel drums. "Local lore claims this is one of the houses built by ships' carpenters," Harry said. "You are supposed to observe that it has the lines of a sailing vessel."

"Looks like it's all roof," I said.

"That was to catch rain for the cistern," he explained as we emerged from the pines. "On top, that little widow's walk was for spotting wrecks to plunder. Paul built the house from old plans."

At the back of a three-level deck wrapped around a kidney-shaped pool strewn with orange hibiscus blossoms, three ebony men in tight flowered pants over bare weightlifters' torsos bonged out a tune that I recognized but couldn't name. Under strings of Japanese lanterns on the second level, two bored-looking women in tight white jeans switched exercise-conditioned hips to the beat as they stared into some zonked-out distance. We walked past a wood-and-mesh cage, taller than my head, that was aflutter with cockatoos, against which a tall woman had backed a red-haired man for a private moment.

"Am I the only man wearing socks with his loafers?" I asked Harry, and then, when he only answered a knowing smile, "Which one is Marge?"

"At an air show," he said, "where do you go?"

"Usually the hangar. Where the pilots and the mechs are."

Harry nodded. "Marge is probably in the kitchen."

A beach boy wearing a glowing tan and not much else offered us squid wrapped in seaweed. Harry introduced me to a brush-cut woman wearing a silver coke spoon necklace, a dour Latino with a drooping moustache and a row of earrings and then to the host, Paul Armond, a round little man with a shiny bald pate and a permanent expression of happy surprise. I said, "Thanks for allowing a tourist into your beautiful party."

Squeezing a moist handshake, Paul said, "A friend of Harry's is an honorary conch."

"But it's still a good idea to keep your hand on your wallet," Harry said.

"How do you get to be a real conch?" I asked.

"One of only two ways," Paul said. "Born one, or born again. Baptized in my pool."

He reached out to stop a passing man with a gray ponytail caught in some kind of a beaded clasp, saying, "Remember, pot limit."

The man said something I didn't catch but I noticed, on one pumped-up bicep, a tattoo of a shell with a suggestively shaped pink mouth. As we drifted away, past two more cages, one with love birds and the other with what I thought were macaws, I asked Harry, "You notice the porno tattoo?"

"I think it's supposed to be a conch," he said, "but you can use your imagination. I was glad to hear Paul setting a pot limit."

"He wasn't talking about a poker game?"

"I don't think so. I think he was saying, 'nothing harder than marijuana.' Sounds like he's setting house rules."

At the bar, three topless teenagers – one boy and two girls – poured frozen daiquiris into frosted stemmed glasses. "I know you weren't born here," I said, "so you must have been baptized in the pool."

Harry laughed. "More than once. But not tonight. You stay as long as you like, but don't be surprised at anything after midnight." He pointed to the pool. "See those hibiscus flowers? That's the baptismal costume. Three for the ladies and one for the gentlemen."

Then, waving his daiquiri at a woman who was spearing a charcoal-seared shrimp from a passing tray: "There she is." He towed me by my free elbow past a couple of men in muscle shirts as she half turned toward us, leaning forward to keep shrimp sauce from dripping on what I thought must be a linen shift. I caught a momentary impression of seal-brown hair styled into a close-fitting cap and a face with a little too much nose, and then Harry was introducing me as a g-suit pilot who was learning to be a cook.

Marge Landers fluttered a gesture that said she needed time with her shrimp, asking a question with her eyebrows. "He'll explain it to you," Harry said, waving to someone else and holding his glass over his head as he dodged back through the crowd.

With a cocktail napkin she mopped what was perhaps a little too much chin and said, mock-solemnly: "G-suit – that a formal g-string?"

"It's what a military pilot wears. Not me any more."

"Grounded?"

"Retired."

"So you're learning to be a cook?"

"Trying to discover what I want to be when I grow up. I saw a magazine article about a gourmet cooking school and decided to start there."

She snared a glass of champagne from a passing tray and said, "Let me guess – Villa dé Licosa?"

Surprised, I said, "That's it. Don't tell me you've–"

She shook her head. "I've just read about it and dreamed. Don't tell me how wonderful it was – I'll get bitchy."

"Food was starchy and the view was those ugly Tuscan hills. Afternoons we visited boring places like Florence, Sienna and the Chianti wineries."

"Must have been grim. But you love to cook in spite of all that?"

"So far. But I don't have an instrument rating yet."

She smiled. "Great cooks don't measure. They taste."

She looked around at a burst of laughter from a group sharing a joint at the edge of the pool, giving me the opportunity to study her face. She'd probably been called "horsey" as a child. Now, approaching middle age, the oversize features and prominent cheekbones melded into a look of style shaped by the soft cap of dark hair, and she wore the loose shift with the casual ease of a model. The shapes and planes of her face caught the light when she looked away, as if to pose for a hidden camera.

I made conversation: "Harry says that without you, Margaret's is a loser."

"When I was running it, *I* was the loser." And then, "Now I'm going to check out the buffet before these people wreck it. Paul said he wants me to rate his new caterer."

I fell into the buffet line behind her and she made conversation: "How long will you be with us in Key West?"

On an impulse I said, "I'm supposed to leave tomorrow. If I miss my plane, could I see you again?"

"Of course not. Man who can't make a flight – what would you call that? Responsibility challenged?"

As I filled my plate with potato pancakes topped with smoked salmon, Cuban-style shredded beef, a pasta tossed with scallops in pesto sauce and a salad of mangos and pears, I noticed that she was taking little samples of everything. When we reached the dessert table she said, "How would you rate this buffet?"

"I'd say–" I thought for a moment, aware that this was a test question "–lavish but uninspired."

She smiled and nodded. "The avocado salsa is interesting. "Hint of jalapeno and cilantro."

I pressed: "I'd miss the flight with a responsible purpose. To pursue a new career."

She glanced at me under an arched brow as she led me to a table where two gray-haired men were talking to girls who looked like their daughters. After the introductions she said, "I'm doing a buffet survey – what are the winners and losers?"

"Great daiquiris," one of the men said.

"Speaks volumes for the buffet," Marge said. "Anything else?"

One of the girls said, "Key lime pie isn't bad."

"Now there's a surprise," Marge said. And then to me: "I think there's more bad key lime pie served in Key West than anywhere else in the world. Our claim to fame."

Our table mates leaned their heads together to hear something one of the men said sotto voce about "Joe weed trouble" – I could guess what kind of weed he was talking about – as Marge asked me, "What career have you decided to pursue?"

"Think I might like to be a treasure hunter."

She pursed her lips and nodded, mock-solemnly. "Lot of rich divorcees get off those cruise ships."

The two teeny boppers laughed in harmony – one soprano and one alto – to something audible only on their side of the table, which caused me to notice that Marge had yet to laugh in our conversation. She'd smiled, nodded, raised an eyebrow – used a full repertoire of conversational expressions – but she hadn't laughed. The thought made me aware of the continuous female party laughter rising and falling around us like part of the background music. Women talking to men.

"Promise not to laugh?" I said.

"Promise."

"I'm thinking about looking for lost treasure at sea."

She put her hand over her mouth as if to suppress a laugh. "Really," making it a statement.

"Sounds like a kid's fantasy, doesn't it?" I answered. "But yes, really."

"I think I know what sort of man hunts treasure in lonely bedrooms, but–" she turned a gesture that left the question unsaid.

"I'm asking myself that very question. First, what sort of a woman opens a restaurant?"

I traded a taste of her pie for a taste of cherry tart that, we decided, had too much corn starch. Instead of answering she asked, "When you land on an aircraft carrier, how fast are you going?"

"Little over a hundred miles an hour." I noticed that her seal-crop hair had rust highlights.

She raised her brows and stared at me, absorbing that. "Hundred miles an hour," she repeated. "And you hook some kind of a cable, right?"

"It's a controlled crash, every time."

She acknowledged someone across the pool and then, when she looked back: "Why'd you retire?"

"Wasn't my idea. Problem is, we won the cold war."

She shook her head, mock solemnly. "What a shame."

"When I made captain, the Navy had five hundred and thirty five ships. Now they have about three hundred, and all the rear admirals they need."

The two May-and-November couples excused themselves and giggled off to the bar. "Only the pursued, the pursuing, the busy and the tired," she said, watching them.

"That's got to be from something I haven't read," I said.

She smiled one of her vocabulary of expressions, this one self-deprecating. "Scott Fitzgerald. Last word on big phony parties."

I said, "Question pending on the floor: what kind of a woman opens a restaurant?"

"Business school graduate. Wants to be an entrepreneur instead of a corporate bureaucrat."

"Why Key West?"

"My ex is a hedge fund manager. He had a client who retired to Palm Beach. Josh – he's my ex – he went down on business, met some other retired folks with money to invest. We decided that south Florida needed a money manager with new ideas, and Key West needed a restaurant that didn't cater to a cruise ship clientele."

"Sounds like a good plan."

She waved to someone across the pool and stood up, leaving her plate only sampled. "It was. Husband and restaurant were both great successes. Both are now operating without me, of course, but–" she flipped a farewell gesture "–business plan can't cover every detail." As she moved away she said, "Thanks for helping me critique the dinner. And if you do miss your plane, good luck in your treasure hunting career."

Trying to maintain the connection, I said, "That job, it's cooking. Cook on a treasure ship."

That made her pause. "A cook – on the strength of that Villa dé Licosa course?"

"That, and sea legs. I've got plenty of shipboard experience. But I may need some advice on provisioning my galley. Could I call you?"

She looked around and picked up a match book from an empty table. "Got a pen?"

Cycling home I told Harry that, if his condo wasn't rented, I'd like to stay a couple of days longer and see what the Jolly Roger ad is all about. Maybe have another go at the permit and the bone fish.

"You can have it for the rest of the week. Also going to have another go at Marge?"

"Thought I might. Just to figure out how you can get her back to Margaret's. Cover my rent for the condo." I didn't say anything about the woman on the beach.

Thinking about that now, as I looked down into the parking lot by the moped rental place where the cops had parked their white Mercury, it occurred to me that, after what I'd told them, Marge was sure to be questioned. I went inside, found the matchbook with her phone number and called. When her machine answered I said, "This is Burke Bascomb, bearer of bad news. Maybe you already know, but your friend Paul Armond was found in his pool this morning. The police were just here and I'm afraid they'll be coming to see you too. They want to talk to everybody who was at the party, and I gave them your name. Sorry to load you into the gun, but yours was about the only name I remembered. Price you pay for making such a lasting impression. I'll call you again."

Then I called Harry. He was in a meeting but I asked the secretary to interrupt it for a police matter. When he picked up I told him what I knew and the line was silent for a moment. Then he said, "Can't say I'm terribly surprised. I'm sorry – I liked Paul – but I'm not really surprised. He liked – you could meet a rough crowd there. Paul seemed to think that gave his parties, I don't know, some kind of an edge, I guess. Excitement. You see anybody there that looked like, suspicious?"

"What does suspicious look like?"

"Well, maybe somebody dealing?"

"Saw a joint being passed around. Mostly I just took care of business."

"Business?"

"You told me to see what it would take to get Marge back to Margaret's."

"You found her interesting, right?"

"Just trying to earn the free rent."

"Oh–" as if that reminded him of something "–the D and B I ordered on Jolly Roger? It came in today. They seem legit. Privately held, so they don't have to disclose financials, but they pay their bills and have no liens or litigation. You still planning to answer that ad?"

"Not doing much planning these days, but I'll see if the autopilot takes me there."

CHAPTER 2
Jolly Roger

In Virginia it would have been called a shotgun house: tiny, with one room behind the other. Here it was a conch house, and it also had a wide porch under a shingled overhang supported by skinny, square wooden columns and slatted wooden "blinds" that I'd call shutters except that they were hinged at the top and propped open at the bottom. Over the front door was a sign announcing Jolly Roger Treasures, Inc. with a skull and crossbones logo. But one eyehole of the skull was winking, as if to say that this venture is just a gag, or a lark.

I went into a tiny front room that was furnished as reception office except that it had no receptionist, just an empty desk under a reproduction of an antique chart labeled **Waters and Soundings of the Spanish Main**. On the desk was a PC with a screen that said, *Welcome to Jolly Roger Discoveries Inc. Sign in please.*

I looked around, wondering if this is some kind of a promotional come-on. Prints of galleons on the walls. Prospectus on the hatch-top coffee table. Surveillance camera over the door leading into the next room.

I leaned over the reception-desk keyboard and picked out *Burke Bascomb.*

The screen responded: *Are you here for (click on one):*
Scheduled appointment?
Employment?
Sales?
Other?

I clicked on *Employment?* And the screen asked: *Please complete this brief application:*

Address:
Phone and e-mail:
Employment history:
Marital status:
Education:
Briefly, what else would you like to tell us about yourself?

I entered the address and phone number of Harry's condo on Duval Street that and, for an employment history: *U.S. Navy, retired as captain after 30 years active duty.*

After *Marital status:* I entered *divorced.* I hesitated, thinking about adding *still friendly* or some other phrase attempting to characterize what, at the time, I had thought was a growing-apart but now recognized had never been a marriage. At its best, for me it had been an extended shore leave party. For her, it had been a series of military towns, afternoons of bridge and bloody marys with other bored wives at the officers club among men on shore leave. In the face of boredom and temptation she knew, without ever accusing or even asking, that I wasn't passing up every female opportunity that came my way and so she must have decided, why not? I decided there was no way to convey any of that in a phrase and went on to *Education:*

Public schools in Norfolk Virginia; U.S. Naval Academy, 1966-1970; various military graduate schools, including flight training and Naval War College. As an afterthought I added: *Villa dé Licosa Gourmet School, Ripoli di Lari, Italy.*

Now, what else would I like to say about myself? That I suspected answering this ad was just another way to avoid reality? That after fifty years of trying to live up to expectations and following orders, now I'm trying to discover what I want to be when I grow up? I entered: *What kind of a grown man* becomes a treasure hunter?

The screen dissolved to gray and then: *Roger will be with you shortly. Click here if you'd like to know more about Jolly Roger Discoveries, Inc.*

I clicked, and got:

THE JOLLY ROGER STORY

Under contract to the U.S. Navy, in 1976 Roger Morosoff developed a software package for interpreting sonar images. He then founded Morosoff Enterprises, a company that develops advanced Navy sonar applications and derivative, unclassified software for interpreting medical sonograms and seismic images.

In 1997 he took his company public, and in 1999 he retired as CEO. He continues to consult in the development of new programs and applications.

In 1988, when newspapers reported Tommy Thompson's discovery of the treasure ship Central America using a towed, side-scanning sonar sled, Roger began to think about how Morosoff software could be applied to deep water searches for lost vessels. He investigated that in the same systematic way he had investigated other markets. After several years of feasibility studies, competitive analyses, historical research and preliminary technology tests, in 1998 he organized a corporation with a small number of private investors to explore selected sites outside U.S. territorial waters. One of the investors is Morosoff Enterprises, which will own all software developments and have access to all test data. The other investors, who are all individuals, will own everything of value recovered from the ocean floor after expenses, which include a specified share for the crew.

ALL undersea recovery operations are conducted in a way

to protect historical artifacts. Discoveries are first carefully photographed in situ *both with video and still cameras. If possible, fragile artifacts are recovered in seawater containers. Investors understand and accept that recovery delays and additional costs are necessary to preserve the historical value of discoveries.*

For information about the search techniques, click here.

I clicked, and the screen flipped to:

SEARCHING A FOREIGN MEDIUM

Air is the medium of light, but water is the medium of sound. Dolphins and whales use hearing as we use sight – and more. They perceive shapes and textures, and also interior features, such as fetuses. Cameras are maladapted to subsurface work, where light must be imported. Our search doesn't depend on cameras and light. Instead, we –

"Captain Bascomb, I'm Roger Terrell."

As he showed me into a dining room that had been converted into an office, I got the impression of a small man whose gestures and bearing expanded the space he occupied. He had a tousle of red-blond hair, a spatter of freckles and shoulders that connected to his ears like a collegiate wrestler's. He pointed me into a barrel-backed oak chair facing his chrome and steel desk, which was bare except for an opened laptop. He took his chair under a chart of the Florida Keys thumb-tacked to a cork board on the wall, and I noticed that, although his waiting room walls were decorated with an antique chart and sixteenth century sailing ships, his office was state-of-the-art.

I decided to establish some turf. "Before we get started, why does the skull wink his eyehole?"

He tilted his head back and laughed, as if I'd said something witty. "Positioning strategy," he said. "What's the first thing a treasure hunt needs?"

"Treasure?" I guessed.

"That's the last thing. Before that is the site. Many's the slip between site and ship. But first comes investment. I guess that's treasure too – priming the pump. Before we can start looking we need a some people willing to put up four or five million bucks."

"And that's something to wink at?"

"The wink is marketing. We tell a prospect that he's going to have some fun with this investment. If he can't afford to risk a few thousand bucks for fun, he's not a prospect."

"So you're not really serious about it? Finding treasure?"

He hitched forward in his chair. "Deadly serious. Those of us doing the search – nobody who's not serious is going to grub around out there in a converted barge poring over sonar returns for months at a time. But for the money people, it's just a high-risk gamble. Like a few thousand shares of an IPO – they all do that occasionally. But this is also something they can have fun telling their friends about. If I tried to make a treasure hunt look like a rational venture, they'd laugh."

"But you really–"

He made a sweeping gesture. "There're two hundred years of treasure wrecks out there. Mel Fisher vacuumed up most of the easy, shallow water sites. Tommy Thompson is working at eight to ten thousand feet with high tech technology. My niche is between them, using mostly off-the-shelf hardware with my proprietary software. That's the sweet spot. And when I hit – not if, but *when* I hit – my investors will realize a big return on chump change. For them. And they've already had something to talk about at the club."

He sat back, a smile working at the ends of his broad mouth, and then he made a handing-off gesture toward me. "Are you an investor, Burke? Or are you working for one of my investors – making a reality check?" And then, reacting to my reaction: "The only job I have open is the cook's, and I know you're not applying for that."

"How do you know that?"

The smile broadened. "Come on. Retired Navy captain. Gourmet cooking school. You're not interested in ten hour days aboard a barge. Cooking and washing dishes and listening to the crew bitch about the food."

His candor prompted me to say, "What I'm looking for is some time out. Get used to not being in the Navy, think about what I'm going to do next. But I need to be busy while I do it."

Roger considered that a moment and then, with an apologetic gesture: "You understand, every now and then we get a guy who's not what he says. Maybe wants to know where we're going, or who's backing us or – treasure is a paranoid business."

"You want references?" I asked.

He shook his head. "It just wouldn't work. Not in the galley. I need somebody–" he tossed a 'for instance' gesture "–who's cooked on a merchant ship. Or an off-shore oil platform."

"Not an amateur, you mean."

"I've got nothing against amateurs. We're all amateur treasure hunters. But the cook is our morale officer." He hitched forward again. "You gotta understand. Sonar scanning is boring, tedious work. The boat's rolling, there's always a diesel smell – meals get to be the big thing. I've got to have a cook who knows how to build a meal out of powdered milk and canned goods for a dozen men in a two-by-four galley."

"One thing I do understand is shipboard life," I said. "And scuba. I've clocked plenty of bottom time." And then, before he could break in: "This place have a kitchen?"

"You could call it that. I don't use it."

I looked at my watch. "How about an audition? Give me an hour to shop and hour in your kitchen and let's see what kind of a dinner I can put together with powdered milk and canned goods."

Roger put his head back and laughed again. "You carrier pilots are pretty cocky, aren't you?"

"That's all about confidence," I said.

"I'd enjoy having you along, Burke. Somebody to talk to – most of these computer weenies are half my age. And finding a ship's cook down here–" he shook his head. "I think half of all Key West men wear lavender striped neckties, and men who can cook–" he waved an inclusive gesture "–probably ninety-nine per cent. I've got nothing against gays, but putting one into a jam-packed fo'cs'l for weeks of high pressure living – hell, I wouldn't consider a woman for that job, either. You'd be a great shipmate. But not in the galley." He raised one finger, to signal an idea. "How about – would you consider a special assignment?"

"What kind of assignment?"

"I told you we get guys coming around, sometimes trying to find out something? Guy last week tried to hire me for a dive."

"Hire you?"

"Not me personally. What he wanted was for me to assign an experienced diver to help him locate a wreck. Offered five hundred dollars a day."

"You want to assign me?"

Roger laughed and shook his head. "I don't know anything about this guy. I sure wouldn't put anybody under water with him. But he was wearing what he called a doubloon." He pointed to his neck. "On a chain. Said he knew where there's more. It wasn't a doubloon, but it did look like it might be an old gold coin."

"He let you look at it?"

Roger shook his head. "Said he never takes it off except to dive. Guy's probably a flake. Didn't look like a diver to me."

"Out of shape?"

Roger looked away, as if calling up an image of the doublooner in his mind's eye. "Wasn't that. He's a big guy, little bigger than you are. Could have been a tight end. But he was just so neat and pressed, and he had this thick black moustache that looked like it had been trimmed with a straight-edge – you know what a moustache does to the seal of a scuba mask?"

"No, but I can imagine."

He pointed to his throat. "And he was wearing a cravat. A nice silk paisley cravat. When is the last time you saw an American wearing a cravat?"

"Can't remember the *first* time."

Roger nodded agreement. "And that coin he was wearing–" he shrugged a gesture that said, who knows? "But there're five thousand wrecks out there. Anybody in the water might stumble onto one of them."

"You want me to find out where he got the coin?"

"That may be too much to expect, but I'd like to know anything you can find out. If he's got somebody making day-trip dives for Spanish gold around here, that's interesting."

"If the doubloon guy has found a wreck, then isn't it his?"

He shrugged. "Probably not. If it's in territorial waters it belongs to Florida. But I'd still like to know about it." He looked away into the middle distance, choosing his words. "You see, the treasure ships usually ran aground in a storm. Ship was being blown around. They'd hit a reef, tear a hole but wash off on the next surge. Maybe they'd go for miles, spilling cargo. Sometimes they'd break up – aft section would go down but the forward section would float a while. Sometimes one little reef happened to be in just the right place and three or four ships hit it. You get wrecks all around a site. So–" he turned palms up in a "who knows" gesture.

"So this guy's coin–"

"It could be a fluke, or a fake. But it could be a data point." He pointed to his laptop. "We've got eight years of historical research. Dozens of ship's tracks translated into GPS grids. A new data point is worth–" he shrugged "–probably nothing. But it *could* be worth days of scanning."

"So what would you want me to find out?"

Instead of answering, he said, "Jolly Roger is an enterprise of stakeholders. Crew gets piddling wages, but everybody has a stake in the recovery. Works out to about three and a half per cent per man. Course, I couldn't give you a whole share. But maybe a pro rata share, like Billy."

He waited for me to react, as if assessing my interest, before he explained: "Billy flies a float plane. Mostly takes out sightseers, but he also scouts for some of the fishing boats. If we need an oscillator or a new compressor, or if somebody's got to get to the dentist, we can radio Billy. Usually he'll come. When he does, he bills his day rate and we also credit him a pro rata share of the recovery. If the search and recovery takes a thousand days and Billy flies ten times for us, then he also gets one per cent of the three and a half per cent of a crewman's share."

"Pretty small number," I said.

Roger grinned and nodded. "Tiny multiplier. But Billy thinks we just might find something so rich that–" he waved a gesture "–hell, none of us are in this for wages."

"So if I worked ten days to find out what I can about the doubloon man–"

Roger nodded. "You'd earn a pro rata share. On top of expenses – we'll cover those. I'll give you a letter of marque."

"What's that?"

"Technically, it's contract. But we gussie it up to look like the contracts the privateers got. Specified how much of the loot they could keep." He waved a dismissive gesture. "It's like the Jolly Roger logo – helps keep the adventure in the enterprise."

I thought about that. With Roger I felt the potential for the kind of low-risk camaraderie I'd enjoyed in years of ready-room associations. The kind of guy who can tell a joke and hold his drinks. I felt sure that Roger would have that sense of boundaries that made a friendship comfortable. Now that I was adrift, I was tempted to take his offer just to maintain the connection. But I decided that was a cop-out. "Not my kind of thing," I said. "I'd like to be your cook, not your snoop."

Roger nodded, as if not surprised at that reaction. "Not asking you to peek through any keyholes. Just watch for a boat named *Dutch Treat*. Guys around the fishing pier say she was chartered by the doubloon guy."

"Sport fisherman?"

"The boat is. But the captain – all I know is they call him Dutch – he sounds like a boat bum. Whatever fishing he does is probably mostly for square grouper."

When I shook my head he explained: "What the locals call bales of marijuana. The boats from down south throw it over the side when they see the Coasties coming. Washes ashore, and some of it is still smokeable. Which means saleable. Anyway, I think the doubloon guy may have chartered *Dutch Treat* as a private dive boat."

"Sounds like you've already made some inquiries."

"Couple of–" he wobbled an ambiguous gesture "–discrete questions. Don't want to signal that I'm interested."

"Why don't you send Billy out to look around?"

Roger raised one hand to wave that idea away. "There's probably thirty sport fishermen out there on any given day – maybe more – and they all look alike from the air. You know that."

"So you want to hire me to ask some stupid tourist questions."

He smiled. "Let's say, innocent questions. You wouldn't have to ask about the guy, or even the boat. Matter of fact, I'd rather you didn't. There's a treasure psychosis, you know."

"No, I don't know."

"The idea of treasure, it makes some people–" he pointed a finger at his temple and drew circles in the air. "For openers, just ask about the woman. Any tourist might be interested in her."

"You didn't tell me about a woman."

He shrugged. "She arrived with the Doublooner, but she doesn't go out on *Dutch Treat*. He goes alone with Dutch. But what I'm told, anybody who sees that woman is going to remember her."

"You know this woman?"

"Only by description."

"She have a touch of the Orient?"

He pointed a "that's it" gesture. "You've seen her too?" he asked.

"Saw a woman walking the beach. And yes, I remember her. What do you want to know about her?"

He turned both palms up. "Anything that might give us a clue to the Doublooner. You'll think of something. But don't say anything to connect you with us."

I hesitated, wondering if she walked the beach every day and, if she did, how I might approach her. I remembered that I had the match book with Marge's phone number. Had I promised Harry that I'd see her again? Sort of. Roger tapped some keys on his laptop, and I heard a printer wind up. "Let me show you our letter of marque," he said.

I thumbed a gesture toward his waiting room. "When I signed in on your machine I asked what sort of a grown man becomes a treasure hunter."

Roger stood and went to the printer in the corner. He returned with two sheets of paper, glancing over them. "A treasure hunter?" he said. "In my case, treasure's more interesting than golf, or playing the market. Some of the crew..." he shrugged "...probably running from routine. We're all infected with vivid imaginations." He slid the contract across the table to me. "And I suppose we're all looking for something. The treasure's our excuse."

CHAPTER 3
Push Your Luck

In the fifth grade I waited after school to walk home with the girl with blond banana curls. When she appeared I didn't know what to say, and so she walked home alone. Waiting now on Fort Zach beach, I still didn't know what to say. According to Roger, I'd think of something.

Two days ago I'd seen her on the beach at about nine in the morning, and so today I was there a little after eight. I had the beach to myself as I went through my stretching and bending routine and then started jogging along the solid damp sand just below the line of tidal wrack. In the harsh subtropical sunlight, the idea of waiting for a woman I didn't know for a clue to where a man I'd never seen might be diving for a treasure seemed preposterous. Was it something I'd seen, or imagined, in those exotic eyes in the moment when she took off her sunglasses and looked directly at me in the shade of the pine? Or was it the telephone number Marge had written on the match book that was now in the bedside table drawer at Harry's condo? Or was it a touch of treasure psychosis, the lure of excitement and big money?

Money had never been the driver in my life and now, after my wife had been considerate enough to dump me for a man of means, my captain's pension and a small portfolio inherited from my father, the first and probably last Bascomb admiral, was providing what I needed for some self-assessment and transition planning. But eventually I'd need some earned income. I decided that even a small share of a treasure site could make a big difference in my outlook.

I'd finished my two-mile jog and was still hanging around at nine thirty, feeling increasingly foolish, when she appeared, wearing the same floppy hat and teasing coverup. As I watched her striding along the edge of tidal wrack the connection closed: tidal wrack. She didn't walk at the same time every morning, she walked at the same *tide*. Low tide. But she didn't scavenge the tide for shells or critters; she walked an invisible straight line to an inaudible march beat.

And then, as if she had heard my thought, she paused, turned, went back to a tide pool she hadn't seem to notice, retrieved something that dangled from thumb and forefinger, carried it to the water's edge and tossed it into the gentle curl of surf.

I stood and walked out of the pine shade to meet her. "Let me guess," I said. "You rescued a stranded starfish."

She took off her sunglasses. Enigmatic Oriental eyes considered me a moment, as they had the first day. "He was still alive," she said in a rich contralto with no hint of the sing-song East.

"Kindness to the starfish but bad news for the clams."

She put the glasses back, concealing her eyes. "Clams? How could a little starfish hurt a clam?"

"Overpowering affection." I made a hugging gesture. "Wraps his arms around the clam and squeezes. After a few hours the clam can't keep his trap shut. Then he's dinner."

"Hours?" she said.

"Patience is rewarded."

"Always?" It seemed to me that she managed to suggest a lot with a single word.

"Among the starfish and the clams, probably yes. On dry land, I'm not sure." I started to say something about her appearance rewarding my patience but thought better of it and settled for: "Mind if I walk with you a ways?"

She seemed to consider that before she said, "Yes."

I took that to mean "okay" and turned to start down the beach, but she didn't move.

"I'm sorry," she said. "Yes, I mind."

I took a step back with an embarrassed "Oh, I – I only–"

She stopped me with an open palm. "This is my solitude. This time on the beach. It's my zen. It – feeds my spirit?" The intonation asked me to understand.

"Of course. I don't mean to intrude."

"And I don't mean to *be* rude." She smiled, making the rhyme a little private joke.

As I started to back away she said, "Wait just a moment." She took something from a wallet inside the mesh bag slung over her shoulder and held it out to me. "Here is my lucky chip. Maybe it will bring you luck too."

It was a two dollar token from the *Sunset Cruise Casino*. I tried to hand it back. "I can't take your–"

She held up her hand to stop me again. "Please. I want you to have it."

"You're not going to play again?"

Her laugh was incongruously rough, a blues chuckle. "Oh, I'll play again."

"Then you'll need your lucky chip."

She shook her head. "Luck doesn't work like that. Luck is like love. You only get it by giving it away. If you win with the chip, then you must give it away. To someone deserving." She waved goodbye and started down the beach. After a couple of steps she glanced back and caught me watching the action. "You deserve my chip for the starfish and patience. Something to think about as I walk."

Instead of going back to the empty condo, I drove past the

wrecks along houseboat row, hoping to spot *Dutch Treat* somewhere in the harbor. When I came to the charter boats I parked and walked over to the pier to see if I could strike up a conversation with someone who might know the boat.

A skinny, sun-blackened youngster with a Latino accent in ragged cut-offs and a "Show Me Your Tits" tee shirt called up from the cockpit of *Top Hook,* "Got an open rod for this afternoon. A I hesitated, remembering that my contract with Roger included expenses. "Hundred bucks for some Gulf Stream action," he said. "We took big jacks this morning."

I decided I'd get more information as a charter customer and signed up for the one o'clock departure. I had time to watch the welfare tarpon drifting under the pier waiting for handouts at the Turtle Kraal while I enjoyed a dozen oysters and two draft beers, and when I got back to *Top Hook* the five others were already aboard. They seemed to all know each other and all had single-syllable nicknames like Mac and Al that I forgot as soon as I shook hands. The captain wore his sun-streaked sorrel hair in a Prince Valiant cut and looked down from the flying bridge through wrap-around sunglasses. His permanent half smile seemed an expression of detached amusement at the behavior of tourists.

As we stood out of the harbor I sat on the gunwale at the knee of the stern while they organized a twenty dollar pool on the biggest fish. We passed a couple of sport fishermen on mooring buoys, but I couldn't read the names on their transoms.

On the way out to the edge of the Gulf Stream we stopped twice at patches of floating debris that had created miniature food chains, at the top of which were small mahi mahi that would take bucktails on light tackle. When we got into blue water the mate rigged trolling lines and I gave Al or Nick or Joe – one of the monosyllables – my seat so that I could climb up to the flying bridge and talk to the captain.

"You ever take out wreck divers?" I asked.

His permanent smile widened. "Shit no."

I waited.

Eventually, he gestured down toward the cockpit and added, "Enough trouble when they're in the boat. I don't want nobody in the water."

"Understand," I said. "You know – what about the other captains? Any of them take me out?"

"Nobody I know." He turned, studied the ballyhoo baits skipping beyond the wake and called something incomprehensible to the mate, who nodded, popped one of the lines off an outrigger, brought the bait in half a dozen turns and pinned the line back.

"How about a captain named Dutch?" I tried.

The fixed smile collapsed. After perhaps half a minute of being ignored I pressed: "Somebody told me Dutch would take a diver out."

"He's no captain."

"Heard he operates a charter boat."

"He's got a boat but he's no charter captain."

"No license?"

"No nothing. Boat gypsy." When he glanced over at me the half smile was back in place. "None of us–" pause to check the baits again "–we don't know him."

"But he takes divers out?"

"Talk to him." The captain turned to watch what was happening in the cockpit, which was nothing. After looking at his back a while I understood that this tourist would get no more information from him.

When we landed I tipped the mate and left the others posing for pictures with the jacks they'd caught while I went to the phone booth on the corner of the pier and called Sunset Casino Cruises. The recording told me that "we sail at six, serve dinner on board, return at midnight, charge twenty-five dollars boarding fee and you keep all your winnings." Sure.

I checked my watch and decided I had time to call Marge. When she answered I said, "Would you believe? I missed my plane."

"Decided to pursue your treasure hunting career?"

"Matter of fact, I've been hard at work on it all day. Just came ashore. But I'm running into some them-and-us. You know, us conchs and them tourists."

"On the treasure boat?"

"No, it's – I'd have to explain. But first, I'm sorry about putting the cops onto you."

"They'd have gotten around to me sooner or later. And I'd help them, if I could. Poor old Paul."

"What do you think happened?"

"Well, I don't think he went for an early morning swim. All kinds of people come to his parties. Came to them. They could get – you know, mostly it was just skinny dipping and smoking and snorting, but maybe something got out of control."

"Cops seem to think so. But the reason I called – how would you like to taste some of what I learned at Villa dé Licosa tomorrow?"

When she didn't answer immediately, I pressed: "Harry's condo has a toy kitchen, but I could stir up a pasta if you could bring a salad." Again, I filled the pause: "It's not just any pasta. It's a Tuscan experience. And I'll show you how."

"What's the address?"

At six o'clock that evening I boarded the *Sunset Casino* up an aluminum gangway that led onto the fantail. Forward, through the windows in a pair of saloon-style doors, I could see dealers setting up for the evening. I followed half a dozen others up the steel stairs to the top deck under a stretched canvas sun shade. A bartender was tapping a keg as a trio tuned two guitars against an "A" repeated on an electronic keyboard. I wandered around, watched the crowd around a juggler on the Mallory Square pier, looked into the vacant pilot house – stainless steel wheel and throttle levers, GPS screen glowing over a chart table cluttered with cups and ash trays, radar shaded with a black hood – all the time checking the new arrivals as they approached the gangway.

What if I'd misread the gift of the lucky chip? If she wasn't planning to gamble tonight, then I was looking forward to what would surely be a forgettable dinner and four hours of trying to enjoy slowly losing a couple of hundred dollars, which I'd set as my limit.

The dock hands were singling up the lines at seven o'clock when she came striding along the pier in that same purposeful rhythm I'd watched on the beach. She was again in white, this time a loose blouse over toreador pants with some sort of a medallion necklace and her hair tied into a pony tail with a white silk scarf. Oblivious to the nudges and glances in her wake, she handed her ticket to the purser who signaled to raise the ramp as if he had been waiting for her.

The horn bellowed a "backing" signal and the trio struck up "Anchor's Aweigh." Gamblers lined the rail as the warehouses began to slide past. I bought a beer and leaned on the bar with the lucky chip in my hand, trying various greetings in my mind's ear as I waited for her to come up. When we were beginning the turn into the channel and the trio segued into "Red Sails in the Sunset" rendered in a hiccuppy rock beat, I realized that she must have stayed on the fantail. I walked over to the aft rail to look down, saw that the casino had opened and decided she must be inside.

I finished my beer and watched the sunset. Had she gone directly into the casino to meet someone? Maybe the Doublooner. I'd seen her, but she hadn't seen me. Might be useful to keep it that way for a while.

The others began drifting downstairs, and by the time the boat began figure-eights at the edge of the three mile limit I was alone with the trio and the bartender. I had another beer to be sure the casino was in full action and then I went down and pushed through the saloon doors.

Inside, the low overhead was painted silver and incongruously stamp-patterned like a colonial tin ceiling. The carpet displayed dingy faces of kings, queens and jacks. Slot machines lined three bulkheads; the cashier's cage and a bar filled the fourth. A craps table, roulette wheel and four blackjack tables enclosed two pit bosses in shiny business suits. The tables were tended by five women and three men, all in tuxedo shirts with scarlet bow ties. Two cocktail waitresses threaded through the crowd.

I dropped my lucky chip on the "pass" line at the craps table and looked around, trying to spot her. The shooter, a lady with white hair as perfect as Mozart's wig and a diamond that glittered when she shook the dice, rolled three consecutive passes. After the second pass a couple of side-bet players cheered and the "pass" line got crowded with chips. I pulled two chips back and she crapped out, to loud groans, leaving me six dollars up.

I drifted out of the noisy excitement of the craps table into the dour concentration of blackjack and there she was, at the twenty dollar table. From across the pit I watched her split eights, catch a jack in one hand and ace in the other to win forty. Three hands later she doubled down on seven-deuce, looking at a six in the dealer's hand. Without changing the permanent smile on his soft round face he dealt her a five, but then dealt himself a jack to bust.

She nodded, tossed him a twenty dollar tip and exchanged her chips for what I guessed must be hundreds, which she dropped into her little white shoulder-strap bag as she stood and started through the crowd toward the doors onto the fantail. After a moment I followed her.

She was standing at the rail, watching the bow wave spreading past. I joined her and held out the chip. "I won with it and so now I have to give it away. Are you deserving?"

She flashed a smile, quick as a surprised child, but she didn't take the chip. "Giving it to you brought me luck tonight. I'd be afraid to take it back."

"I saw you double down on nine. Thought you were pushing your luck a little."

She turned away from the rail. "When your luck is running you have to push it, don't you think?"

"Not in my business."

"Which is?"

"Was, actually. I was a pilot."

She tilted her head as if to see me better. "There's no luck in that business? I thought pilots were–" she made a swooping gesture.

"Some are. There're bold pilots and there are old pilots. But there are no old, bold pilots."

She chuckled that blues-singer laugh. "You make that up?"

"No, and neither did the flight instructor who told me."

"Probably no rich, bold gamblers either." She took a step away from the rail. "I've had my breath of fresh air – now I have to get back to the table."

"Do you have your car at the pier." I asked. When she raised her brows I explained, "Or could I give you a lift back to your hotel?"

"I don't have a car *or* a hotel. We're boat people. I just call a cab when we get to the dock."

"Then I could drop you at the boat basin. It's on my way."

"On your way? You must be in Old Town."

"Flagler. Friend of mine let me use his condo for the week. I've been sort of a boat person too, most of my life, but temporarily I'm in a penthouse."

"So push your luck – enjoy it," she said with a little wave as she went back through the saloon doors, leaving me to wonder whether I would drive her back to the boat basin or not.

Dinner proved to be an adequate buffet that included a broiled local yellowtail snapper that was only slightly overcooked and some stout shipboard coffee, which occupied me until eight fifteen. Back on the action deck it took me a couple of hours, making small bets at the craps table and then at the five dollar blackjack table, to lose my two hundred. I kept away from the twenty dollar blackjack but glanced over at her when the dice were passing or my dealer was shuffling. She sat parade-ground straight, both wrists on the edge of the table, making tiny "hit" or "stand" gestures with the fingers of her right hand and never taking her eyes off the cards. Once I saw her exchange three stacks of blue twenty-dollar chips for three orange-striped one-hundreds, but I also saw her buy some twenties back and so I couldn't estimate how much she might be winning or losing. At about ten thirty I went back up to the top deck where a dozen or so other losers were drinking and trying to talk over the noise of the trio. By the time I finished a beer the boat had stopped making figure-eights and steadied up on a course back toward the loom of Key West. I went back down to watch the last-bets excitement.

At the craps table, three young brown men were whooping and moaning as they covered the side bets for each roll. When one ran out of chips he peeled three hundred-dollar bills off a fat roll to buy more, and I remembered what Roger had said about square grouper. It occurred to me that a gambling boat would be an ideal laundry for money.

She was playing with the same expressionless concentration, but instead of a couple of chips she now backed her hand with a short stack that looked like a hundred, or perhaps a hundred and twenty. I watched her lose one hand, win the next and then, on the last hand, she bet two stacks and won. She gathered up her chips and tipped the dealer sixty. As he leaned over the table to say something into her ear, I noticed the way his curly hair was styled into a modified pageboy where it met the collar of his tuxedo. She nodded understanding and went to the cashier's window.

As I threaded through the noisy crowd, most of whom I knew had to be losers, I recognized some of the same tension-release hilarity of flight crews after a mission, and it occurred to me that tension release is part of most kinds of pleasure, which prompted the thought that I was developing a palpable tension of my own that had nothing to do with risking a couple of hundred bucks.

I drifted with the crowd through the swinging doors that someone had clipped open against the bulkhead, onto the fantail and then up the steel steps to the top deck where the trio, playing now for tips, whanged out a nasal rock-a-billy. Watching the traces of luminescence spreading in the wake and speculating about how many millions of tiny lives our passing disturbed, I didn't realize she had joined me at the rail until she said, "Is the ride home still open?"

"Least I could do in exchange for the lucky chip."

She sipped at something in a plastic bar glass, enigmatic eyes studying me over the rim. "I don't believe you played enough to have any real luck, good or bad."

"No? And I didn't think you were paying attention to anything but your own hand." When she only smiled I went on: "I didn't hit my limit until about half an hour ago."

She dipped her head in a little bow that spoke of the Orient and said, "You set limits, then. In all things?"

I didn't know how to answer that, and so instead I asked, "How about you – ahead?"

She waved a "yes-and-no" gesture. "A little."

"Better than being a little behind."

"Not for me." She looked away, into the wet wind that fluttered her black ponytail. After a long moment she turned back, smiling at whatever she had been thinking. "You see, I don't set limits. That's my sad story."

"Financing some losses, other nights?"

"You could say that, yes. Financing some big losses."

"I noticed that your lucky chips went to one of the dealers tonight."

"Arthur? I always tip him, win or lose. I want to stay in his game."

I knew the pit boss moved dealers from one table to the next every few minutes and so I must have given her a puzzled look. She explained: "Arthur runs a private game on his day off. It's really–" she flashed a smile "–worthwhile. Pot limit. But tell me, what do you mean that you are a sort of boat person?"

I told her I was third generation Navy, and when she asked how I got the name Burke I explained that my grandfather named me after Admiral Arleigh "Thirty One Knot" Burke, whom he served under in World War II. In the course of that conversation I learned that her name was Gisu and that she was living aboard *Happy Daze* with a friend. When I said I'd heard that her friend was a treasure hunter she gave me a look as expressionless as if she were reading her blackjack hand and said, "Isn't everyone?"

I hesitated, wondering if she was telling me that she somehow knew I was associated with Jolly Roger, but then she added, "I mean, isn't everyone searching for his treasure?" and walked away to drop her plastic bar glass in the trash can, closing that subject.

When she returned she seemed interested in my explanation of docking a ship as the conning officer surged ahead on one screw and back on the other in a roil of foam and sediment and then tweaked the ship's drift with the thrusters. We waited for the first press of people to clear the gangway and then we went down. At the bottom she said, "When we get to the boat basin – let me off a block before, okay?"

"Wherever you say. Someone waiting up?"

She glanced back at the ship, and following her eyes I saw a man leaning on the rail, apparently watching us. "Probably not," she said. "But Doubles – you never know."

"Doubles? That's really his name?"

She turned up both palms. "That's what everyone calls him. Joey Doubles."

I started to ask if that was why he wore the doubloon but caught myself, remembering her deadpan, assessing look when I said I'd heard that her friend was a treasure hunter. Instead, I asked, "You just stopping over in Key West?" I looked back again at the man against the rail. I couldn't see the doll face and painted smile, but I thought I could make out the curly coiffure. Yes, I felt sure, it was Arthur, the dealer.

"We're on our way north," she said and then, again changing the conversational course: "What's it like living in a penthouse?"

I told her about fishing with Harry as a way of explaining why I was at the Flagler, but I didn't say that after Harry left I was staying another week to go treasure hunting. When we got into my rental car and started out of the lot Gisu said, with a new edge to her voice, "Remember – let me out before we get to the boat basin. Up the street and around the corner, okay?"

"You have a dinghy or something on the beach?" I asked.

Her answer was an ambiguous monosyllable, and the tension in her posture – hiked forward in the seat with her left shoulder turned to me – told me that she wanted no more conversation. When we came to the intersection of Duval and one of those cross-streets with women's names she twisted around to face me.

"Here." A whisper, as if someone might overhear. "Let me off here."

When I pulled over to the curb she had the seat belt off. She leaned across and brushed her cheek against mine. "Thank you, son of the son of the shipmate of Thirty-one Knot Burke. And remember, life is not all careful limits." Then she put her hand on the back of my head and kissed me on – and, momentarily, in – the mouth.

Quickly out of the car, she said, "Turn around here and go back. Don't follow, okay?"

"Of course not. I know my limits."

But when she turned the corner toward the beach I switched off the ignition and walked down the narrow sidewalk, stumbling over the ridges heaved up by banyan roots, to the corner where I could see the beach.

In the smear of moonlight across the flat calm bay she was rowing what looked like an inflatable boat toward the vague shape that I knew was *Happy Daze* swinging on her mooring.

As I watched a shadow moved on the flying bridge.
Someone was waiting up.

CHAPTER 4
Target Fixation

The next morning I bought the *Key West Sentinel* from the machine in front of the 7-11 on my way to breakfast and learned that low tide was at 10:58 AM. Plenty of time, I decided as I pedaled down Caroline past the Frederick Douglas Community Center and the conch houses with shutters propped open at windows with peeling frames. I could enjoy the pecan pancakes served on picnic benches under the huge spreading fig at the Blue Heaven and still get down to the beach before the tide turned. But, when she came along, looking for solitude, then what?

I decided to leave the lady to her zen. After breakfast I fed my pancake leavings to the street-wise black-and-bronze chickens that scratched through the mulch around my toe-thong sandals, walked back to the Flagler and called Harry. This time the secretary put me right through. Harry opened with, "So, did your autopilot take you to the Jolly Roger?"

"It did, but I didn't land the cook's job. You're now speaking to Trenchcoat Burke."

When I told him about my assignment he said, "I don't know, Burke."

"You don't know what?"

"I don't know whether that's a good idea. You know what your problem is, don't you?"

"Somehow I think you're going to tell me."

He made an impatient little noise. "How many times have I already told you?"

"I know," I said. "We don't have to win the war all by ourselves."

He pressed: "And what is your problem?"

"Target fixation."

"Say it again."

I repeated: "My problem is target fixation."

"And what may be the consequences of that problem?"

Picking up our established, before-mission litany, I responded: "Young widows."

"And how does it work?"

"When we have a mission, I do not break off the attack until we have hit the target."

"And that is courageous?"

"Sometimes that is stupid. We fly a twenty million dollar airplane to lay ordnance on little men carrying their own sacks of rice. Our first job is to bring the airplane home."

"The airplane?"

"The airplane, with you and me in it."

"All right," Harry said, "you remember. At least you can still say the words."

"What does that mean?"

"What that means," Harry said, "is this trenchcoat mission – that sounds pretty stupid to me. I keep thinking about Paul. Everybody in town knew him and liked him. You've got to believe he was getting into something I don't know."

"You think maybe he was involved in some kind of treasure hunt?"

"Whatever it was, he – look, just watch your step down there, Burke. Don't get target fixation, okay?"

After we hung up I got into my rental Chevy and drove to the boat basin. Most of the boats were out, but the kid in the "show me your tits" shirt was still trying to fill a chair aboard *Top Hook*. "Not today," I said. "But do you know – what's that boat out there on the mooring buoy?"

He looked around, and then: "Whatta you mean, what is it? It's a sport fish."

"I mean the name. Is that the *Dutch Treat*?"

He shook his head. "She's out. That's the *Happy Daze*."

From what I could see she had an ocean-going deep-V hull with a comfortable beam and a graceful sheer line. "Nice boat," I offered. "She for charter?"

"Shit no. Tourist boat."

"A couple?" I pressed.

He grinned. "Gotta be the dumbest somebitch in town. Goes out diving and leaves prime quiff running loose. You see her, you'll know what I mean." And then, to a passerby behind me: "Hey, I've got a chair open for big jacks, mahi mahi and maybe a sailfish if you're lucky."

I drove to the supermarket to shop for tonight's dinner with Marge. Pushing the cart down the aisle and considering what would be the appropriate wine, I found myself wondering why anyone would leave a nice sea boat like *Happy Daze* on the mooring and charter another sport fisherman to dive for doubloons. And, as the man said, leave prime quiff running loose.

Browsing through a surprisingly varied collection of table wines I remembered that Marge had chosen champagne at the party. That would be the safe call. Then I recognized the label of a winery I'd visited. Chianti Classico would be right with pasta, and something Tuscan would provide a conversation peg. On the way to the checkout I paused at some greenhouse tulips, but decided no, fresh flowers would be trying too hard. Instead, I stopped at the Book Revue, found F. Scott Fitzgerald and bought a copy of *The Great Gatsby*.

Back at the condo, from the meager collection of CDs Harry left for his tenants I selected some Oscar Peterson and Dave

Brubeck that, at low volume, would provide neutral background.

Why was I being so careful? We were just two grown-ups having dinner to talk over a project. But when she buzzed from the lobby I hurried to the speaker as if she might get away.

Instead of a bowlful of salad, Marge stepped off the elevator with a grocery bag. She was wearing a simple peasant blouse over a full skirt in a geometric pattern with a three-strand necklace of heavy stones and pottery shards. As I showed her in she announced, "First, I want to look around. I've never seen a penthouse."

Harry's place was furnished in standard up-scale timeshare: faux Casablanca fans, faux Spanish grills on windows and doors, fat wicker furniture with pillows in tropical prints, pottery lamps and floral watercolors in painted frames. Marge stopped at the one personal touch, an enlarged snapshot in a brushed steel frame over the wine rack in the dining room. "What's that?" she asked.

"Picture I shot when we were fishing the flats last year. Harry calls it 'Journey's End.' I call it 'Transition.'"

"But what is it?"

"Boat wrecked on a sandbar. Those are mangroves growing out of it. Seeds drifted into the wreck, and now they're converting it into an island."

"Transition." She nodded. "You always take the long view?"

"Hardly ever. I guess transitions are on my mind these days," I said, leading her back to the kitchen. "The best feature is the terrace, but I want to save the effect for dinner. You can hear the air conditioners on the roof, but the view is worth it."

Marge's grocery sack was full of arugula, bib and romaine lettuce, with a bottle of complicated-smelling dressing and a little jar of salmon and cream cheese on the bottom. While I was looking for plates that would do for hors d'oeuvres she poured two glasses of the Chianti I'd opened and put them out of reach on the dining room table saying, in a gotcha tone, "It doesn't breathe in the bottle, you know – only in the glass."

While we washed, tossed and dressed the salad, I talked about learning to use a maxa luna knife to chop the onions, celery, carrots and garlic for wild hare in wine. Moving around the transient kitchen we brushed elbows and hips in an intimacy that, in some way I couldn't define, seemed closer than on a dance floor. We talked about cooking and the Villa dé Licosa and how I happened to go there, which opened the subject of my retirement and divorce and learning to fend for myself, which opened the subject of her divorce.

"We were both twenty-four seven people," she said. "Pagers and cell phones went to bed with us, to the bathroom – everywhere. We took Melissa – she's our daughter – we went on vacations to Europe and Belize. And we went to her recitals and school things. We were keeping two careers and a family on track all at the same time. That's what we thought. Salad's ready. Now we can try that Chianti."

When I showed her through the sliders onto the terrace she stood for a full minute, looking around the lights of the island. "Key West, I love it, but–" she started, and then backtracked: "I mean, it's a funky place. Tacky, and fun. Except when something awful happens, like poor Paul. But from up here, it's – magical."

"First time I ever flew an airplane," I said, "I thought, this is the God's eye view."

"But you got over that," she said.

"Not really. Not completely. Over here – Harry's got a telescope."

She experimented with the knobs, not asking for help, and then exclaimed, "Wow. Takes me right up to Hemingway's door. And there's Mel Fisher's – been through there? It's for the tourists, of course, but there're some real artifacts – oh, is that – yes, that's the corner of Paul Armond's pool." She came back to sling chair next to mine. "I don't want to think about poor old Paul."

Which gave me an opening to change the subject: "What happened to the two careers and the family?"

She propped her feet on the pipe railing, tilted the stem glass, sipped, rolled the wine around like mouthwash, pursed her lips and nodded. "On the back of the palate. Can't taste the oak, but a hint of what? Cherry?" And then: "One day Melissa didn't come home from school. Called us that night from Nassau."

She turned away from the panorama of lights to fix me with a level gaze that assessed how I was taking this in. I don't know what she saw, but after a long pause she went on: "Josh and I were thrilled."

"Because she called," I said, trying to offer empathy. "She called right away."

She set the glass carefully behind the leg of her chair, out of the way of feet. "She was trying to sound blasé, but I could hear the tremble underneath. Said she'd gone on a party with some spring breakers. Truth is, they'd picked her up. Couple of college boys. She was fourteen."

Marge left that hanging in the moist air between us, and I decided not to touch it. After a while she glanced at me with a forced smile that said she was just giving me the synopsis, not the emotions. "Josh chartered a plane, and on the way over I told him I was going to sell the restaurant and I wanted him to make more time for Melissa. And for a while he really tried." She made a dismissive gesture. "But business always had to come first. Don't you think it's time for the salad?"

We collected our glasses and went back inside. I opened the other Chianti while she scooped salad onto the two plates I'd set at either end of Harry's table. I kept the conversation culinary, and we were well into the salad when she volunteered: "Melissa's turning out fine. Connecticut College. Dean's list. Sees more of her father now than she ever did. They live in Darien."

"Josh does," I filled in.

"With his young wife and his baby and his big career."

Venturing onto uncertain ground, I asked, "How do you feel about that?"

She stirred slightly in her chair, as if gathering herself to change the subject. Instead, she fixed me with a level, are-you-ready-for-this? look and said, "I love him."

I must have reacted because she smiled and then explained, "Not Josh. The boy I married. Josh turned into a walking, talking career, but the boy I married–" she paused and shook her head slowly. "Ever know a skier who attacks the mountain? That was Josh." She punched at the air. "That's how he went at everything. He'd max out our credit cards to buy theater tickets and he jogged with a Walkman so he could listen to Mahler. On our first anniversary–" she laughed, remembering. "Well, being young and married to Josh was like being plugged into my own personal booster cable. Today we're co-parents. Cool but cooperative. So – how do you feel about your ex?"

"Not so generous, I'm afraid." I tried to find a way to match her candor. "You were the dumper, I was the dumpee. Makes a difference. But then, well, hell, I had it coming. I know that."

She stood, collecting our salad plates. "That'll do. In my book, responsible trumps generous every time."

I served the pasta, explaining that "pasta puttanesca"

translates to "whore's pasta" probably because it can be thrown together quickly from ingredients in every Italian kitchen after a hard night's work, and when we were seated again she prompted, "On the phone, you said something about a conchs and tourists problem."

I told her about the Doublooner and my deal with Jolly Roger, and then I described how the captain of the *Top Hook* turned me off when I asked questions about somebody named Dutch. "Roger was right about one thing: when I ask questions the locals don't prick their ears up. But they don't come up with any answers, either."

She washed pasta down with a sip of Chianti before she asked, "What exactly do you want to know?"

"Just whether there's any reason for Roger to send Billy out looking for the place where a sport fisherman could be diving a wreck."

"Billy?"

"He's the float plane pilot."

She cocked her head, looking at me under a raised eyebrow. "This treasure hunting – you're actually serious about it?"

"I know, it sounds like kid stuff. But when you talk to Roger, he throws out side scanning sonar and eight years of research and five thousand wrecks – and then there's Mel Fisher and all the stuff he's vacuumed up. And Roger talks about other high-tech crews poking around. He makes it sound like treasure hunting's an industry."

She smiled and shook her head skeptically.

"I know," I went on, "he's a salesman. Maybe a con man. But at the moment, yes, I'm serious about it."

She thought about that. "Josh and I – we still keep the *Bottom Line*."

"A boat?"

"Josh's. He comes down every year for the tarpon run. I keep an eye on the boat for him, and once in a while Melissa and I use it for picnics and shelling. Anyway, I know some of the guys at the marina. I suppose I could ask about this Captain Dutch."

"Just if it feels – you know, don't push anything."

She smiled as she stood up. "The only thing I'm pushy about is food. And your pasta was every bit as advertised. Thanks for the evening."

As I walked her to the elevator she said, "That view from the roof – the God's eye view – I guess that's what got me talking about Josh. I've never done that before. Hope I didn't embarrass you."

"You didn't. But if I was Josh, I'd be kicking myself all the way to the bank."

"For selling out to success?"

"For losing you."

She gave me another of those examining looks, and then, with a smile: "I think you can hold your own with Jolly Roger the con man. I'll let you know what I learn at the marina."

Back in the condo I restarted Brubeck to break the silence and then, after I'd loaded the dishwasher, I turned off most of the lights so that I didn't have to look at the transient decor and used a credit card to put in a call to my son on the private line in his bedroom. Busy. Damned computer quest game. If I was going to get Greg an appointment to the Academy he ought to be doing homework. I thought about calling Harry with a report on the chances of getting Marge back into Margaret's, but realized I didn't have anything to report. Retirement plus divorce equals solitude. Deal with it.

I must have been dreaming about her, because when the pounding on the door rousted me out of bed I heard myself say,

"Marge?" In that first, disoriented moment I thought perhaps I had dreamed the noise, but then I heard the banging again, loud enough to rattle the lock. The bedside clock said 6:28.

As I stumbled through the bedroom door in my Navy boxers and tee shirt I glanced around to establish waking reality: shafts of early sunlight through the vertical blinds at the slider doors, two dead Chianti soldiers from last night on the counter that divided kitchen from living-dining, the "transitions" snapshot next to the desk and then I was at the door. "Who is it?" I called, fumbling with the lock.

A scared voice, like a child's: "Please."

When I got the door open and saw her, eyes wide as a waif's, I said, "Gisu?" asking if this was real.

"I'm so sorry–" her words tumbling over each other "–this is terribly early–" not glancing below eye level "–but I need – I have to – please, may I come in? Just for a moment."

When I stood aside she looked around, toward the elevator behind her, and then went quickly past me into the living room to stand at the sliders, her back to me as I went past into the bedroom. She was wearing the white bikini and translucent coverup that I remembered from the beach.

"Is there some kind of trouble?" I asked through the door as I climbed into some jeans.

"Yes. You could say that." The panicky tremolo was gone, and I even thought I heard an ironic smile behind her words.

I used the toilet, scrubbed the toothbrush around my mouth and ran a comb through my hair. When I padded barefoot out of the bedroom she turned to face me, and sure enough, there was the beginning of a smile. "Do you need help?" I asked.

"Yes," pulling the coverup together in a way that made me notice her body. "I need to be – out of sight for a little while. Do you mind if I use you as a hideout?" She must have seen

something skeptical in my face because she added, with a
disarming smile that flashed small perfect teeth, "Just for a
couple of hours?"

Coming out of the dream, had I imagined the child's voice,
the pleading tone with words falling over each other? To open
some time I asked, "How about some coffee?"

"I'd kill for a cup," she said.

Startled by that extravagant figure of speech, I retrieved the
coffee pot from the dishwasher as she went on: "You did mean
to tell me how to find you, didn't you?"

When I looked up she treated me to that smile again and said,
"On the boat. You told me that you were staying in your friend's
penthouse, remember? At the Flagler."

I started to say I didn't remember offering an invitation but
stopped at, "I remember talking about that, yes."

She pulled a pouty little expression. "You're not sorry to see
me, are you? I mean, it's not too early for company, is it?"
Again she squeezed the coverup together, forearms under her
breasts. And then, teasing: "Outside your limits?"

How many roles did she play? "Who is it you're hiding
from?" I asked.

She tilted her head with that music-hall chuckle. "Not the
cops. Don't worry – you're not abetting a felony." And then,
still smiling, "Not yet."

As I took mugs out of the dishwasher and set them on the
counter I decided to take a stab: "Something to do with a
treasure hunt?"

She moved a little toward me, as if stepping over an invisible
threshold. "You really do have treasure on your mind, don't
you, Burke?"

I temporized: "Everyone is searching for his own treasure.
That's what a wise lady told me."

She laughed. "Wise. If I was wise I'd be gone with it. Not hiding out."

"You have it? The treasure?"

She took another step toward me, put both hands on my chest and gave a playful push. "You don't waste time, do you, Captain Thirty-one Knot Burke? How much do you expect to get for a cup of coffee?"

"Coffee and a hide-out," I said. "Who are we hiding from, Joey Doubles?"

She stiffened, and for a moment the waif was back. After a long, staring pause she said, almost in a whisper, "He suspects that I know. It's making him nuts."

"What does he – you're afraid of him?"

She hunched her shoulders and crossed her arms protectively, hands on shoulders. "I – please, can we have some coffee?"

As I interrupted the half-perked pot to pour a couple of mugs I heard the sliders open, and when I turned around she was out on the roof terrace. I carried the mugs out, finding her peering through the telescope. "Look," she said, suddenly excited as a kid on Christmas. "I can see *Happy Daze*. And *Dutch Treat* is gone."

"What does that mean?" I held out one of the mugs, but instead of taking it she clapped her hands.

"That means they're out. Off shore, diving for treasure. And we can do anything we want." She took a step closer, hands still together as if in prayer. At that range I noticed that she subtly used eyeliner to emphasize the exotic tilt of her large eyes. "And you know what I want to do? Right now? Like the Spice Girls – what I really, really want?"

With another step she was standing between the two steaming mugs, head tilted back to look into my face. She put both hands on the outside of my legs and, showing the tip of her tongue but not taking her eyes off mine, sank to her knees in a graceful, practiced motion. I slopped hot coffee on my wrist as she began to unbutton my jeans.

After a moment I emptied the two mugs onto the terrace duckboards and looked around to make sure that the only windows higher than Flagler penthouse belonged to an F-18 lining up on final approach to the Naval Air Station. When Gisu finally stood up, I stepped out of my jeans and shorts and left the coffee mugs behind on our way to the bedroom.

I'm not proud of it, but in the many ports-of-call I've visited, I've *been* visited by a few call girls. I remember every one, but none was like Gisu. Not remotely. She was skillful beyond anything I remember or could have imagined. At some point, when I'd caught my breath, I asked, "God, where did you learn that?" and she said, "In the best little whorehouse in Ho Chi Minh City."

Much later, when I'd had to ask for a recess and she was massaging my neck and shoulders, her fingers discovering and dissolving tension, she said, "You must have all your thirty-one knots in just your shoulders. Why are you at war with yourself?"

"Only war I have left."

"Was it awful, being in the war?"

"I suppose the right answer is yes," I said, "but the truth is, no, not for me."

"You liked the danger?"

"The challenge. I liked that. Flying combat is technical. You have to do things just exactly right, and that's interesting. A challenge. You also have to have some luck, and that's exciting."

"Like gambling. But killing people, wasn't that awful?"

"We didn't think about it that way. For us it was missions, and targets to take out. Somebody else made the big decisions. We didn't have to worry about whether this was the right war. It was our war, that's all. What we'd been trained for."

"It didn't have any purpose, the war?"

"They told us it was about containing Communism, which seemed like a good idea. But all that was way above my pay grade. I just didn't have to worry about it. I didn't even have to worry about the target – whether it was worth the risk. But once you're in the air you're absolutely your own boss. I liked that a lot."

"And the people in the target – they were just slopes, right?"

I said, "You're Viet Namese?"

"Half," she said, giving me a playful slap on the butt and sitting back against the headboard. "Mother was a working girl and Daddy was a GI. We don't know which GI, but obviously one with some Africa in his genes."

"How did you wind up with Joey Doubles?"

"He bought me." She smiled at my reaction. "Happens a lot. GI daughters don't count for much there, especially if you're part black. Joey Doubles appreciates a good whorehouse education and so–" she turned over both hands with a shrug and that sweet smile "–what the hell, it beats working the street."

She reached over and ran her fingertips teasingly down my belly. "What about you, Burke? You interested in lower education?"

"What's the tuition?" I asked.

"Just room in your bed. I can pay my own way."

"And Joey Doubles – isn't he a problem?"

She sat up and measured me with another of her long assessing looks. "Nothing we can't solve."

"You said he thinks you know. You mean, where the

treasure is?"

She chuckled that provocative laugh. "He and that stupid Dutch – they're swimming around down in the dark right now, while we're up here having a penthouse party."

"They're not going to find it?"

"Not if we take care of business."

"What kind of business, Gisu?"

She leaned over and nuzzled my neck. "Your business," she said in my ear, "is taking out targets, right?"

"It was."

Still in my ear: "Targets worth the risk."

When I didn't answer she straightened up and said, conversationally, "Joey Doubles is an evil man. And what he's looking for should be mine. Could be ours."

When she saw the look on my face she laughed and rolled out of bed. "Just something to think about. In case you ever get lonely."

She wriggled into the bikini bottom and then, before she put on the top, she shimmied everything into motion and skipped out as if dancing off stage.

I thought about going out onto the terrace to retrieve my pants but decided to wait and see what might happen next. I heard her move through the living-dining room. Then silence. I remembered that we'd left the sliders open and imagined her out on the roof, scanning the harbor through the telescope to make sure the *Dutch Treat* was still off shore. Just as I was beginning to wonder if she could have slipped out without my hearing her, she appeared at the bedroom door.

"What does it mean, thirty-one knots?"

"That was what he said – the Admiral. When he got orders to engage the enemy he'd radio 'Am proceeding at thirty-one knots.' You see, everyone knew Burke's ships could only make thirty knots."

She nodded, smiling. "That was his way of saying to hell with the limits."

"Something like that."

"If you could say to hell with the limits … just one time." She blew a kiss. "I'll be trying my luck on the *Sunset* tomorrow night. Think about it."

CHAPTER 5
Shipwreck Party

The sun was baking the terrace when I pulled shorts and jeans back on, made a quick telescope check to confirm that *Dutch Treat* was still out, found the two mugs I'd emptied and dropped in that startled moment when Gisu showed me what she "really wanted to do" and went inside to refill one of them from the remains of the pot. Nothing, from the moment the pounding on the door jerked me out of a dream of Marge until now, when I was trying to understand what I was feeling, seemed real. Not the carnal acrobatics, and certainly not the proposition that I buy out her love slave contract with – what?

"Your business is taking out targets," she'd said. "Targets worth the risk." The idea seemed preposterous, but was there any other possible interpretation? No, Gisu wanted me to take out Joey Doubles. An evil man, she'd said. "Don't worry – you're not abetting a felony. Not yet." I was thinking of Gisu standing in the bedroom door and taunting me about limits, when the telephone rang.

"Special agent reporting in from the marina," Marge said. "No problem getting answers, one conch to another. The doubloon guy and his hybrid beauty are the talk of the seawall."

"What are they up to?"

"They're diving, all right. Don't seem to have any experience, though. Couple of weeks ago the guy took the scuba course. You know, what they sell to the tourists who want to try diving. And then the two of them went out on the *Happy Daze* a few times. Since then the guy's been going out on *Dutch Treat* and the lady's been staying ashore."

"What do you make of that?" I asked.

"I'm just the sleuth. You're supposed to deduce the deductions."

"Is Dutch an experienced diver?"

"That I didn't ask. He's not local. How would the guys at the pier know that?"

"Probably wouldn't. You know anybody who'd rent me an off-shore boat?"

"Know some guys who'd take you off-shore, on a charter. But nobody's going to turn their boat over to somebody they don't even know."

I stood and carried the phone over to the sliders, where I could see the harbor with *Dutch Treat*'s empty mooring. "I sure would like to know where they're diving, but I don't want to alert any of the charter boat skippers."

Background hum on the phone for a moment, and then Marge said, *"Bottom Line*'s twenty-eight feet. I wouldn't want to take her to the Tortugas, but a few miles off shore – we've had her out there plenty of times."

"You'd rent her to me?"

"Couldn't do that. Josh wouldn't – I just couldn't do that. But maybe I could take you out."

"Thanks, but that's probably not a good idea."

"She's a Cape Dory. Deep V with plenty of beam, pilot house open to the cockpit but no flying bridge."

I hesitated, tempted. "No, I don't think so. But thanks."

"You don't trust anybody, do you?"

"It's not that." I tried to explain: "Roger talks about treasure psychosis. Makes people do weird things."

"You're afraid I'll catch it?"

"No, I think those people – the doubloon guy, and Dutch – I think they have an acute case. I don't want to take you along on a snooping trip, because I don't know what they're capable of doing."

"We'll take fishing rods. Anybody sees us, we're trolling jacks."

I couldn't think of a convincing argument short of saying that this was sufficiently serious that I'd been offered a hit contract, which would have required explaining how that had come about. "Marge, I just don't want to involve you."

"But you already have, haven't you?

In the end, she agreed that if we spotted *Dutch Treat* we'd just troll past and not try to get close for an accurate position fix, and I agreed to be on the pier at six o'clock the next morning, which would give us time to get out before first light. When I arrived, the harbor was breathing mist and Marge already had the boat off the mooring and alongside an empty finger pier, engine guttering and burbling when the slight swell dunked the exhaust. In the moist hush she murmured "Welcome aboard" as I cast off and hopped into the cockpit.

She cranked the wheel and slipped the engine into gear, shoving just enough way on the boat for steerage with no wake. I noticed that she hit the right throttle position the first try and turned slightly into the running tide to crab straight up the channel. I stayed in the cockpit, trying to pick *Happy Daze* out of the vague shapes swinging on moorings as we stood out through the channel lights. Once I heard the squeak of oar locks and thought I saw a dinghy, which could have been en route to *Dutch Treat*. When we were alongside the jetty, the boat rolling slightly in the first ocean swells, I went forward to stand next to Marge at the helm.

The red instrument glow carved dramatic planes in her face as she peered through the salt-streaked windshield. Condensation dripped off the overhead, and she'd slipped a yellow foul-weather jacket over her white shorts and tee shirt.

I and asked, "You see a weather report?"

"Heard the marine radio," she said. "Forecasts seas two to four beyond the reef."

"About as good as it gets off shore. Where's the wind?"

"The usual. Northeast off the Gulf Stream, variable eight to twelve with occasional local showers and gusts."

"Standard south Florida?"

She nodded. "For this time of the year. Where do you want to go when we get past the jetty?"

"North is mostly shoals and mangroves, right? They'll probably turn south, toward blue water."

She thumbed a gesture over her shoulder toward a drop table in the corner of the pilot house. "There's a chart under the plexiglass. I'll turn south and hang around until we see them go past."

When the sun began to streak orange, red and indigo highlights into the bland fluffy cumulus stacked on the horizon, I selected two rods from the overhead rack and rigged them with plastic squid. As I let the lines out to trolling range Marge called back: "If you get a fish on, are you going to be able to cut him off so we can keep up with *Dutch Treat*?"

"We'll see. Proof of character." I mounted the rods visibly in the holders and sat in the fighting chair, glancing back from time to time at Marge, who was watching the inlet through binoculars as she kept the boat in a constant slow turn.

When the sun was clear of the horizon she took off her jacket. As I moved forward out of cockpit I noticed the nape of her neck, showing now just below the severe cap-cut line of her hair, and it occurred to me that I could understand how Japanese men find that vulnerable little hollow erotic.

"What are the symptoms of treasure psychosis?" she asked.

"In my case? Embarrassment. I keep asking, am I really

doing this?"

"How about your friend Roger?"

"He acts like this is just a business venture. Like – opening a restaurant. Lot of work and a certain amount of risk, but worth it if you plan carefully and have a reasonable amount of luck."

"Sounds rational enough."

"Oh, I think Roger's plenty rational. Rational to a fault. Wants to check out every possibility. It's the doubloon guy – he's the treasure-wacky one."

"How do you know that?"

I hesitated, groping for an answer that avoided telling her about my encounter with Gisu. "Well, first he tries to hire a diver, and then he goes to scuba school and now he hires a guy they call a boat bum to take him out. I think he's got doubloons on the brain," I finished lamely.

"Here comes a boat," Marge said, peering through the binoculars. "Go sit in the chair and hold a rod."

It proved to be a charter boat with a cockpit full of fishermen. During the next ten minutes, two other charters rounded the jetty and turned south. Then Marge said, "I think this may be the one."

She held the heading and I stood up to make sure I was clearly visible with the fishing rod as the sport fisherman went past. I noticed a stumpy gin pole guyed to the flying bridge and rigged with two blocks for lifting sharks, and then, as they turned south, even without the binoculars I could read *Dutch Treat* on the transom. I looked around at Marge, who nodded and began straightening our heading onto theirs.

As she eased more way on the boat I cranked in the lures and then, with the rods back in the holders, I went forward into the pilot house. Marge had the throttle full and *Bottom Line* was throwing spray as she slammed into the swells.

"Running dead into the wind," she said. "That sport fisherman's got more weight and freeboard than we have."

"Probably more horses, too," I said. I looked at the compass, trying to get a bearing on their heading, but the ball was wobbling and swinging back and forth so much that the best I could read was an approximate one point west of south.

"Try to keep them in sight," I said. "You have a GPS?"

She nodded and flipped a switch above the windshield. An overhead screen came alive, displaying a string of numbers. After a few more tooth-rattling minutes she throttled back and picked up the binoculars. "I don't see them any more," she said, steadying one elbow in the corner of the pilot house. After a moment she handed the glasses to me.

I scanned the horizon slowly, trying to keep alert to my peripheral vision. When I put the glasses down I looked at the compass. "Come right a few degrees. If they're anchored we ought to be able to find them."

I went back into the cockpit where I could scan the horizon abeam on both sides, leaving her to watch off the bows. The porpoising ride over the dead-on swells reduced my vision to a series of glimpses, and we were almost past before I saw the boat. "Come right," I yelled. "I think I've got her off the starboard quarter."

Marge swung around. Porpoising changed to rolling as we took the swells on the beam. "Wind seems to be freshening," she said.

I grabbed the binoculars. "I'm pretty sure … it's a sport fish about the right size. And I see an anchor ball … but no red pennant with a white slash."

"You wouldn't expect them to advertise their dive site," Marge said. "Burke, nobody's going to think we're trying to fish in this stuff."

"You're right, this is close enough. Let's head for the barn." I found a ball-point pen in the holder behind the chart table. Searching through my pockets for a piece of paper, I settled for a dollar bill and copied the numbers off the GPS screen onto George's forehead. Then I went back to the binoculars and the anchored boat.

Marge had instinctively turned off the wind, which drifted us closer before we steadied up and started running down the seas. Through the glasses I could see activity in the anchored boat's cockpit.

I looked around the horizon. Those puffy cumulus clouds that had been so beautifully side-lighted by the sunrise had collected now into an anvil-topped thunderhead, and the seas were breaking off scraps of foam. I lurched forward into the pilot house and said, "Let's see how fast this thing will go."

"Think they saw us?"

"Maybe. They've got eight or ten feet more height-of-eye from that flying bridge. If they were looking, they'd see us before we could see them."

"Breeze is definitely freshening now."

I nodded. "Looks like weather building. What did you say was the forecast?"

"Eight to twelve knots with occasional showers and gusts."

I looked back over the surging wake at the clouds. "Looks like all of that. Maybe an honest-to-god south Florida line squall."

For perhaps ten minutes we ran down-wind at full throttle, but the squall line was moving closer. Now, as *Bottom Line* crested each boiling sea, she hung for a moment before the propeller dug, and then as she started down the face of the wave the stern settled and the following sea broke over the transom into the cockpit. The scuppers were running full. Marge said,

"Don't know how long I can hold this speed."

"Try steering a point off the wind," I suggested, "so we take those seas on the quarter."

She raised her voice to be heard. "We'll have to come back to get into the harbor."

"I'd rather cut some zigs and zags than swamp her."

She came right a few degrees, which allowed the boat to roll off those crests without taking any solid water. I was looking at the GPS chart, trying to estimate where our landfall would be, when she said, "Looks like they're packing it in too."

I looked back. *Dutch Treat* was perhaps a mile behind us, following in our wake. "Why don't you come back left now," I said, trying for a casual tone. "We can take the seas on the other quarter and not get so far outside the course to the harbor."

I was hoping they would hold their heading and begin to open some separation, but they changed course with us. I remembered Gisu whispering, "He thinks I know. It's making him nuts." After a few minutes I said, "Okay, come back the other way now." When Marge came right they changed course with us again, and now they were clearly closing. "You at full throttle?" I asked.

When she looked around to nod she saw me looking astern. "You think – they look like they're following us."

"Looks like it. I guess they saw us marking their dive site."

The squall line was now visible as a solid wall of rain that seemed to accelerate as it approached. I called out over the wind, which was picking up baritone harmonics, "Squall's going to wash over us in a minute. They won't be able to see us in there."

I looked back at *Dutch Treat* just as she disappeared into the squall line, trying to see if she had a radar antenna turning above the flying bridge. I didn't get a good look, but I didn't see one.

Should have thought to look sooner. "When the weather gets to us," I said, lurching over to the chart table, "you'll probably have to throttle back. Now try to come left again, okay?"

She nodded, spreading her feet slightly like a batter digging in. Peering up at the GPS display, I wrote the numbers on the back of my hand and then, just before the solid impact of the squall arrived, I switched to display to chart and located our position.

As if bursting through a transparent membrane, rain suddenly hammered the overhead. Marge cranked the wheel first one way and then back again to keep from broaching. The surface disappeared in rain and spindrift and the seas seemed confused, coming from different directions, but they only built to five or six feet before the wailing wind knocked off the crests. "You want to take the wheel?" Marge yelled, easing the throttle back a few turns.

I crabbed forward along the coaming to speak into her ear: "You're doing fine." I caught a whiff of a clean, soapy scent with no hormonal musk as I added, "Just keep the seas behind us and cheat to the right whenever you get a chance."

She gestured with her right hand. "Don't we run out of water over there?"

"Not for a ways yet. I've got us on the chart. What does this boat draw – d'you know?"

She shook her head and answered with a question. "Three, maybe four feet?"

"Plenty of water here, but it shoals up fast. I'll watch the GPS. Just don't let us get broadside to one of these."

As the boat started up the face of a wave I looked back into the unblinking eye of a small shark, maybe a dogfish, staring out of the following sea. In an instant it disappeared in a welter of foam, leaving me wondering if perhaps I'd imagined it. I switched the GPS to display our position on the chart.

"These tropical squalls are just local disturbances," I yelled, confirming that we were well west of the harbor entrance.

"So?" she called back over her shoulder. "Right now local is *us*." She twisted around for a quick glance astern. "Why are they chasing us?"

Trying for an off-hand tone I answered, "Who knows? Don't worry – they can't follow us into the mangroves."

"Into the what?"

"Just keep doing what you're doing – keep the waves behind us and keep cheating to the right. I'm tracking us on the chart."

"Did you say into the mangroves?"

I lurched back up alongside her to speak without shouting. "When this blows through they'll probably be way over there..." gesturing to the left "...somewhere. They'll give us up and we can just take our time going home."

She wrestled the wheel, watching the seas over her right shoulder. "Hope you're right. But what was that about the mangroves?"

"That's just a last resort. If they're still looking for us, we can ease back into the shoals. They've got a faster sea boat but she draws more water – they couldn't stay with us back there."

She glanced around momentarily. "You really don't want them to catch up with us, do you? You're really worried about that, right?"

I thought about a forty-two foot sport fisherman ramming us, wondered where the life preservers might be on this boat and then decided not to bring that up at the moment. Instead, I said, "I'm sorry I got you into this."

Without taking her eyes off the water she said, "So am I. Tell me about the mangroves. What *I'm* worried about – I really don't want to run aground out here."

"Harry and I have chased bonefish all around these islands. Fear not – I'll keep us afloat."

She gave me a look of less than complete confidence just as one of those cross-waves caught the stern and twisted us under a curl of breaking water. I grabbed the wheel and helped her get the helm over as the sea broke across the gunwale and the boat heeled, hung for an endless moment and then staggered back around, water sloshing across the cockpit deck. "Famous last words," she said.

"I think the wind may be shifting a little," I said.

"Sure as hell not letting up."

"Not yet. First it'll shift as the squall goes through. Keep edging to the right."

"Toward the mangroves?"

"Trust me."

That elicited a smile. Then she said, "About being sorry – what I meant was, you said it was a bad idea. I'm sorry I talked you into this."

"Just keep a steady hand on that wheel and we'll be fine. And hey – the wind is definitely clocking around to the east."

She looked around. "You think the rain is easing up?"

"Maybe a little. Squall will pass over as fast as it came onto us." I peered at the GPS for another fix and called out, "We're running off the edge of the shoal now. You don't have to keep coming right."

"I gave that up ten minutes ago," she yelled.

The rain changed from drumming the overhead to rattling and then to splashing. The wind no longer tore off the tops of the breakers, but that allowed the seas to build higher. Marge cranked the wheel constantly to keep out from under the water piling up astern as I peered through the binoculars into the thinning rain, looking for the sport fisherman I did not want to see.

Far astern, the sun broke out.

The wind was still keening, the seas were cresting over my head and rain was still sheeting, but behind us rays of light reached for the ocean like one of the miracle paintings I'd seen in Tuscany. Marge was busy meeting and countering the boat's fishtailing. "We're almost out of it," I yelled, and she took one hand off the wheel long enough to flash a thumbs up.

Over the next ten minutes the wind kept shifting and slackening. When the rain thinned out to what I estimated as VFR minimums, I caught a glimpse of a sport fisherman. I braced my elbows on the coaming to hold the binoculars steady as we rode over a crest, trying in that moment before we dropped into the trough to see if she had the distinguishing gin pole forward of the cockpit. I couldn't be sure, but when we crested again they seemed to be changing course. On the next crest it was obvious: they'd come around onto a collision course, which meant it must be *Dutch Treat* and they'd spotted us.

"Looks like it's mangrove time," I said, staggering to the starboard side to look for the islands.

"We'll just run up on the shoal a little way, right?" Marge called.

"There," I pointed. "Broad on the bow – see the two islands? Steer for the channel between them."

"That's going to put us almost broadside to," she said.

"Okay, don't come around that far yet. As we get closer we should pick up some lee and then you can head into the channel."

"We don't have to go clear in there, do we? When we get into four or five feet of water they can't follow."

"I want to get in behind the islands."

"That's crazy. It's knee deep back there."

I turned and, bracing my back against the gunwale, looked over the other side. From the crest I could see *Dutch Treat* pounding through the seas toward us and throwing spray as high as the bridge. "They're popping rivets to catch up," I said.

"Rivets?"

"Airplane talk. Go ahead – turn toward the channel. We'll wallow a little, but the worst is past now."

She cranked the wheel but said, "I don't want to go in there. No need."

I dropped the binoculars onto the neck strap and worked my way forward to stand next to her. "There *is* a need. I don't want them to just stand off and wait for us."

"What's the hurry? Heavy date?"

"I also don't want to give them a chance to look us over."

Her eyes widened, but she kept watching the water.

"So far, they haven't gotten a good look at us," I explained. "This can't be the only Cape Dory in Key West."

She seemed to think about that as she kept the boat surfing down those seas, which were slackening as we caught the lee and the squall went past. After a few minutes sunlight caught up with us, and she said, "This may not be the only Cape Dory in Key West, but I haven't noticed another one."

I changed the subject: "Suppose we *do* run aground. Probably happens all the time. Worst case, we radio the Coast Guard and they send a sea tow for us. Only damage is to our pride."

She thumbed a gesture toward *Dutch Treat*. "What do you think they might do? I mean, if they do catch up?"

"Probably just yell and cuss," I said, sounding unconvincing in my own ears.

"But we don't want to find out, right?" she asked, glancing

back to make sure they were still following. "Aren't we up on the shoal now?"

"Probably. Throttle down to steerage way." I could walk, now, without staggering as I grabbed a towel out of the head, went to the stern sheets and draped it over the *Bottom Line* painted across the transom. "No need to announce ourselves," I explained as I climbed up on the gunwale and started working my way forward.

"Where are you going?"

"Up on the foredeck. Put my two hundred pounds out where it'll lift the propeller a tad, and also where I can watch the bottom coming up to meet us. I'll give you steering signals."

The rain was just a soaking mist now, but the boat was still pitching and rolling and so as soon as I edged past the cabin I got down on hands and knees to work up to the prow. Spread out with my head hanging over, I could catch intermittent glimpses of the gnarly bottom. I held my left arm out, not because I saw any difference in the bottom but just to establish the signal. She immediately turned left, and when I swung my arm around forward she steadied up on the new heading.

As we eased closer to the islands the waves flattened out and I could see occasional keel scars in the bottom among coral heads veined with black lines of environmental stress. She followed my arm signals, the boat just puttering now, along the narrow channel. Something stirred the sand and disappeared again: a flounder, or perhaps a skate.

"They've turned away," she called.

I raised up for a quick look around: one island was abeam and the other was broad on the bow. Roosting egrets speckled the mangroves white. "Too bad," I yelled back. "I thought they might be just pissed enough to follow us in here. Give us the last laugh."

"I can see two guys on the flying bridge. One of them is looking through binoculars."

I sat up again. "Stay in the cabin. Don't let them see you."

"Stay in the cabin? You think this thing is on automatic pilot? You just keep water under the keel." Behind her a frigate bird tilted against a startlingly blue sky.

I looked down again to see a purple fan coral drifting past in the play of surface-wave shadows. I signaled a right turn and craned around for a quick look just before the mangrove island blocked out *Dutch Treat*. The sea stirred with just a light chop back here. Sooty terns skimmed and dived. As soon as I looked down again I could see a ridge approaching.

I twisted around and waved both hands "back." Marge nodded and slipped the engine into reverse just as I felt the thump under my knees. The engine stalled. She cranked the starter, but I shook my head and signaled across my throat, calling: "Let her drift."

We waited. The boat didn't move.

With a smile and a raised eyebrow, Marge said, "You know what my mother told me about men who say, 'Trust me'?"

I stood up and worked my way around the cabin to hop down into the cockpit. "We were going to wait a while back here anyway," I said.

"We were?"

"We want to give them time to give up the chase and go back into the harbor. By then, the tide will probably lift us off."

"What good planning," she said. "The tide is low now?"

"Well, I'm not sure."

"You mean, you didn't check."

I offered my best rueful expression, but she pressed: "Matter of fact, it could be high, right? In which case–"

I held up both hands. "All right. I'll go down and have a

look."

I kicked off my shoes, stripped to my shorts, put my shoes back on, sat on the gunwale and swung my legs overboard. "You might at least look the other way."

"And miss the show?"

When I shoved off the cool water came up to the hem of my boxers. I gulped a breath and swam under the boat. I could see light under the keel – three or four inches of water – but the skeg and one bronze propeller blade were buried in a slight ridge of grainy coral sand. I surfaced and took a step away from the boat to speak to her, standing in the cockpit now. "Come on in – the water's fine."

"We hard aground?" she asked.

"I think I can shove us off. Might help if you'd go all the way forward. But first – you know where there's something I can use to dig with? Like a trowel?"

She thought a moment. "Butcher knife in the galley."

"How about a screwdriver?"

She nodded and went into the cabin. I ducked under for another look. We'd hardly been moving and the impact had been just a tremor under my knees, but the soft sand had swallowed several inches of skeg and half a blade of the screw. I tried scooping sand away with my hands, but it spilled off the ridge like liquid into my furrows.

When I surfaced she was leaning over the gunwale with a rusty screwdriver. I took it and gestured toward the bow: "See you on the front porch."

I heaved a few deep breaths to create an oxygen surplus and ducked under again. Hanging onto the shaft with my left hand, I hacked up clouds of soft sand around the skeg with the screwdriver. When I came up for a breath Marge had sidled past the cabin and was edging along the foredeck. I went down again. Sand was hanging in the water where I'd been working, but the skeg and screw seemed to be buried about as deep.

When I surfaced I studied the exposed mangrove roots a moment, trying to see a high water mark to estimate the tide. I gave that up, tossed the screwdriver into the cockpit and swam forward where Marge was sitting on the prow. To avoid telling her that the skeg and most of a blade were buried, I said, "You look like a figurehead." She struck a pose, leaning precariously over the water, and grinned, as if running aground were not exactly what had been worrying her.

I planted my feet, put my shoulder against the stem of the bow and shoved. After a long while, sparks began to flash in my eyes. My shoes sank to their uppers in the sand. But the boat didn't move.

When I paused, lying back a little in the buoyant water, Marge said, "Isn't there anything I can do besides provide dead weight?"

"Try moving from one side to the other. You know – like rocking a car. See if you can get a rhythm going."

We both moved back amidships, and she began walking from rail to rail in front of the windshield. Each time she went past the centerline toward the other side as I shoved. "Try it a little faster," I said. And then, "Faster," until she was scuttling back and forth and I was heaving with every heartbeat, which I could distinctly hear. But the boat wasn't moving.

When I stopped to catch my breath she sat down, legs dangling over the side. "I feel silly running back and forth. Maybe if we both shove." She pushed off under the rail and splashed in alongside me.

"Hard for both of us to get under the bow at the same time," I said. "Maybe I can lift the stern a little while you shove."

As I swam back I looked at the water level on the exposed

mangrove roots. Maybe a little higher, I thought. Maybe I was estimating with a hopeful eye, but perhaps the tide was rising. I called, "When I yell, give it a shove."

"If you can get it up," she called back, "I can shove it."

I laughed at that as I planted my feet on either side of the screw, my back to the boat, thinking that she was taking this entire fiasco with good humor instead of recrimination. I bent my knees, locked hands under the hub, took a deep breath, yelled "Now!" and heaved.

A grating vibration in my hands. Did the boat move?

Another deep breath, squat, "Now!" and heave. It moved. Definitely.

"One more time," I yelled. "Now!" The hub moved in my hands. I opened them to let the top blade slide through. The stern hit me in the butt. My feet were so mired in the soft sand that I floundered, trying to get out of the way, and shoved the boat back onto the ridge.

I stuck my head under. The skeg was just touching. When I came up I yelled, "Once more."

"That's what you said the last time," she answered, but she shoved – so hard that the boat rocked as it drifted free.

"We're off," I yelled. "I'll hold it here while you get back aboard."

There was a silent moment, and then I heard her splashing along the side of the boat. When she swam up to the stern she let her feet down and threw water out of her hair like a spaniel. "We have a swim ladder," she said. "But of course it's aboard the boat."

We stood there looking at each other a moment, and then we whooped with laughter as if she'd said something brilliantly funny.

I made a stirrup with my hands and boosted her over the

transom, watching her buttocks bunch into well-conditioned muscle under the wet and clinging cotton shorts. She turned around in the cockpit, pulling her soaked and transparent tee shirt away with the thumb and forefinger of each hand. "Look the other way if you want me to get the ladder."

Before I climbed back aboard I towed the boat into five feet of water. I found a snag, led a mooring line under it and back up to a cleat, and then I swam back to the channel between the two islands and looked around: empty water, thrashing in the tail of the squall.

When I swam back to the ladder Marge was wearing the yellow foul weather suit. "Can't see Dutch Treat," I said, climbing aboard. "But they might be waiting for us at the entrance to the harbor. Suppose there's anything to drink in that galley?"

"What is this, a shipwreck party?"

"Sun will be down in an hour or two. I don't think they ever got a good look at us, so let's wait and go in after dark, okay?"

"Only if you put your pants back on."

"Thought this was going to be a shipwreck party."

When I climbed back into my jeans and shirt, wringing the brine out my shorts, she said, "Hang 'em over the port side. My stuff is all over the starboard rail."

"I'll keep my skivvies a decent distance from the Victoria Secrets."

As I was hanging them over the rail she burst out: "Wow – look at that!"

"Just Navy Exchange boxers," I said.

"No – the rainbow. I can see violet, green, yellow, red – and look what it does to the water."

When I hopped down into the cockpit I said, "Short storms make long rainbows."

85

"Why?"

"Maybe because the sun's out while the air's still full of water vapor." I took a seat on the gunwale.

She twisted in the fighting chair to give me a glance. "Captain Prosaic beholds a rainbow." She looked back at it. "I think it's a cosmic apology. Nature's saying, 'sorry about that.' Oh, it's fading already. But look – out there. It's leaving red specks on the water." Then, after a moment: "I think – oh nuts, those are just crab pots."

"You didn't hear it from Captain Prosaic."

She laughed and went to the galley to see if any beer was left over from Josh's last tarpon trip, leaving me to sort out a confusion of emotion. I recognized the juiced-up sense of perception that had lingered after a mission. In the wet light now, the mangrove green vibrated and the egret white shimmered. Looking at the sudden blue sky it occurred to me that this must be how Matisse saw the world, which was an idea as implausible in Captain Prosaic's mind as the colors I was seeing. With a start, I remembered that this was also the effect Gisu had left behind on the beach that first day.

I put that out of my mind and was trying to think of a way to work Matisse into the conversation with Marge when she returned with two cans of Budweiser – I would have expected Josh to stock only imports – and took the chair again. I sat on the transom and we talked comfortably about why the cormorant on a mangrove root knee had to face into the last of the sun and spread his wings to dry, and the shrimp risotto I was planning to try. I'd found the extra virgin olive oil, the plum tomatoes and all the other ingredients except the Carnaroli rice. I'd bought Arborio, which she thought was almost the same.

After a companionable silence, during which I noticed that she didn't need to fill every conversational gap with words and

I decided not to try to impress her with Matisse, she said, "That photograph in Harry's condo. The wreck turning into a mangrove island – you must have shot it back here somewhere."

"Farther back in the shoals. We were in one of those little flats boats – they can float on a spot of damp sand."

She leaned forward in the chair, elbows on knees, and said, "Tell me the truth – why did you really go to that cooking school."

I squirmed a little on the transom and looked away. "Running away," I suppose. "I didn't really think it out. Never really had to do that before. I suppose I just wanted to get clear the hell and gone away from Norfolk, Virginia, and from everything else I'd been doing all my life. My folks live out in San Diego and so I didn't want to head west."

"Your father is Navy too?"

"Retired vice admiral. His father was a chief electrician's mate. My first bicycle was painted blue and gold."

"But why cooking school?"

"Location, location, location, mostly. Only part of Italy I knew was Naples. And what I knew about cooking was nothing. Seemed like a good combination for running away."

"Why not for discovering new possibilities. Do you always put yourself down?"

I managed a laugh. "Matter of fact, I think I usually puff myself up. But shipwreck parties are all about the real you, aren't they?"

She smiled at that and then, to open up a little conversational space, she shaded her eyes to see how close to the horizon the sun had sunk. After a while she said, "Must be a big transition, leaving the Navy. What one thing do you miss the most?"

I thought about that, watching egrets stir the mangrove

island as they settled in for the night. I remembered my conversation with Gisu about the comfort of flying someone else's strategy while being in control of the tactics. "What one thing?" I repeated. "The cat shot, I suppose. Zero to a hundred in three seconds – that's an adrenaline rush. Gotta be the most addictive substance there is."

"Is that why we're running around out here now – an adrenaline fix?"

"If so–"

She interrupted with an erasing gesture in the air. "Sorry. Didn't mean that. This was – I talked you into this. And besides–" her gesture changed to include the sunset "–today turned out okay."

"You mean, I didn't quite manage to sink us. Just got us chased, blown out, soaked and grounded. But we've still got time – maybe I can also get us lost on the way in."

We watched the egrets groom themselves for the night. After a while she asked, "Would it have been different if you hadn't had me along?"

"Maybe not as embarrassing."

She smiled and shook her head. "Ah, the male ego. But you never wanted to take over the helm." She waited a beat, and when I just shrugged she went on: "Josh would have. Come to think, every other man I know would have. Except maybe poor old Paul."

"Now that puts me in interesting company."

"And coming back?" she prompted. "You know, the controlled crash."

"It's all about confidence. The only way you can do it is to know that you're really good at it, because you can't just be close. It's dead-on, or it's a bolter."

She ran her fingers through her damp hair, hesitating as she found the words: "I guess that's how you proved it. Whatever your testosterone had to prove." And then, changing the subject, she pointed over my shoulder. "Look at that."

I twisted around and said, "I think it's a pterodactyl."

"More likely a blue heron," she said.

"Now who's got the prosaic eye?" I pointed a gotcha gesture as I stood up to face the sun. "I'd say we have less than an hour of daylight left. "Probably should move out of here while we can still see. Just in case I find a place to run aground again on the way home."

"Can't do that," she said, standing to go into the cabin. "We're out of underwear."

I climbed up onto the foredeck, retrieved our damp clothes, hopped back into the cockpit, wrapped them in the towel from the transom and tossed them into the cabin. I was thinking about the towel, wondering if I'd covered the name on the stern soon enough, as I uncleated the mooring line and Marge started the engine. I hauled the end of the line back under the snag on the bottom, jerked it free and looked back to give Marge a nod. Then I flaked down the line on the cockpit deck and leaned over the gunwale, watching the bottom sink out of sight as she backed the boat slowly into deep water. When she turned around in the harbor entrance channel I came forward to stand beside her.

"What about *your* transition?" I asked. "Ever miss the restaurant business?"

"In weak moments."

"What would it take to lure you back to Margaret's?"

She shot a raised eyebrow look. "Why?"

"Harry thinks you could turn the place around."

"Harry thinks – you his recruiter?"

"We've been talking about transitions, so what would it

take?"

She leaned over the wheel, looking for the harbor entrance buoy, and the last orange arc of the sun gilded her face into hollows and contours. When she found the buoy and straightened up she saw me studying her. "You could always become a photographer's model," I said. "But I don't think you've given up the restaurant business for good."

"Why do they call it nightfall," she said, changing the subject, "when it gets dark from the ground up?"

"Opposite of sunrise," I said. "In the opinion of Captain Prosaic."

We could see harbor lights now, and music came clearly across the water from someone's patio party. "That's Key West's own Jimmy Buffett," I said.

She smiled and nodded. "You remember. The song's 'Feeding Frenzy' – did I tell you that?"

"No, but I'd say that's a good Key West song subject."

She turned on the running lights and, as we rounded the harbor entrance buoy, backed off the throttle.

"I'd have to own it," she said, without looking away from the channel markers.

"We're talking transitions now, right?"

"You can tell Harry he could be a silent partner, but I'd have to own at least fifty-one per cent."

"Okay, I'll tell him."

"And tell him I'll serve no ranch dressing."

"How about chicken cacciatore?"

She shook her head. "And no penne ala vodka. Or strip sirloin. Been there, don't want to go back."

"So what will be on the menu?"

"Depend on what's fresh that day. I'd want to do all the shopping and look at every dish coming out of the kitchen."

"Sounds impossible."

"That's what you can tell Harry about getting me back to Margaret's. Impossible. See that white light? Our marina. Channel makes a dogleg to the left. Help me spot the markers."

I studied the clots of darker shadow under masthead lights as we went past, and when I thought I recognized the gin pole I said, "Come right a little. Stay over on the edge of the channel."

"Relax," she said. "They're not going to come after us now."

The blur farther out must be *Happy Daze*, I decided, remembering night before last when I'd watched Gisu rowing the dinghy out from shore. I thought of the shadow moving on the flying bridge that night, and again saw in my mind's eye the big man with the prissy black moustache looking through binoculars, this time trying to make out the name on our stern as we muttered past.

Marge laid us alongside the pier with a gentle fender bump. I secured the lines and helped her button up the cabin, noticing that she left nothing adrift. I walked her along the echoing dock and into the dark parking lot where she unlocked an aging bicycle from the stanchions.

"I'll follow you home," I said.

"Don't be paranoid."

"How about protective?"

I tried to read her expression in the half light as she seemed to consider that. "Protective might be nice," she said. "Haven't tried any of that for a long time."

CHAPTER 6
Treasure Psychosis

The next morning I called the Jolly Roger and Roger himself answered. I said, "I've got your data point – now I want to swap it for a piece of the action." We made a date for ten, and when I arrived at the conch-house office he was waiting for me.

I spread out the dollar bill with the GPS numbers on his steel-and-glass-desk and said, "This is where we were. I'd estimate their position about four or five miles northwest, give or take a mile."

Roger took the bill over to the chart thumb-tacked to his cork board and ran his thick finger along one of the latitude lines. "Nothing out there," he said. "Forty to sixty feet of water and sandy bottom. Probably some coral heads, but no reefs or shoals."

"Nothing to wreck a treasure ship?"

He scratched his head, creating tufts of wiry red hair. "Not now. Of course, three hundred years or more can change a lot of bottom contour. And sometimes a stove-in ship could limp a long way before she finally foundered." The wrestler's muscles moved under his tee shirt as he moved his finger up toward the right hand corner of the chart. "You'd assume she was running southwest, with the trades behind her." He shook his head. "Nothing obvious back there." He looked at the numbers on the dollar again, making sure. "If that gold coin came from there, he's onto something I don't know anything about."

"All I know is they sure didn't want us hanging around," I said, and told him about getting chased up onto the flats. "Why don't you send Billy out there?" I asked. "Confirm my GPS numbers. They can't chase off an airplane."

93

Roger pulled an exasperated expression and went back to the chair behind his computer screen. "I'll try, but Billy's getting too big for what he calls 'errand business.' Unless it's a full-day charter, he doesn't want to be bothered."

"If you rent me a plane, I'll fly out there," I said. "But I'm not going back in a boat."

"What about the woman? You talked to her on the gambling ship – you think you could talk to her again?"

"Actually, I did."

His eyebrows went up, and he waited.

"She – came by to see me. Told me the doubloon guy can't find the treasure, but she knows where it is."

Roger hitched forward. "Let me guess. She offered to take you to it for a consideration. Up front."

"Not exactly. She didn't actually offer a deal. Just kind of hinted at it."

"Hinted at what?"

"I'm not sure."

Roger waited.

"Look, it sounds crazy now. Did then, too. But I thought she was hinting that – well, she made it clear that she's scared of the doubloon guy. Joey Doubles, that's what she called him."

Roger made a note on his desk pad. "And?"

"The rest of it she just hinted at."

"She wanted you to protect her from him?"

"I don't thinks that's it. No."

"She wanted you to take him out of the picture?"

"I said it sounds crazy."

Roger stared off into the middle distance, turning the idea around in his mind. "Treasure psychosis. I had a guy come at me with a butcher knife one time."

"Over a share of treasure?"

He shook his head. "We hadn't even found anything. It was just a discussion about hypothetical shares. Difference between a tenth and a twelfth of a hypothetical find. Sometimes, just the idea of a treasure–" he rolled his eyes toward the ceiling.

I put in, "She said this Joey Doubles is going nuts."

"Trying to find it?"

"He suspects she knows where it is."

He pursed his lips, thinking about that. "She could be in a tight spot. You think you could get any more information out of her?"

"Not without a deal. Which I don't want to discuss."

"Think about it. Maybe there's a way."

I stood up to go. "Not for me, there's not. She's a spooky lady."

He stood with me. "You haven't earned a very big share yet. I'd like to keep you involved."

"Better deal me out. I guess I don't want to get involved with a bunch of treasure crazies."

Roger walked me to the door. "Ever visit Mel Fisher's place?"

"No. Never wanted to deal with the cruise ship crowd."

He nodded. "Museum exists to shill for the souvenir shop. But Fisher vacuumed up some wonderful stuff. Hundreds of millions of dollars worth. When you look at all that bloody loot, those cannons that might have fired at Drake or Morgan – makes the Spanish Main with the gold ships and the war galleons–" he raised one thick hand and closed his thumb and forefingers as if to take hold of something in the air. "Well, you really ought to see it before you make up your mind."

"To catch the psychosis?"

"Just keep an open mind. Not every treasure hunt is crazy."

I opted for the liquor store instead of the museum and picked up a Pinot Grigio for my risotto. Then, uneasy at the prospect of hours ahead in my own company, I stopped at the video store for a movie, thinking that I'd had no training for solitude.

The risotto was a success, the movie was a flop and the evening seemed endless. At ten o'clock I changed into shorts and running shoes and tried to jog down Duval past the bars open to the street and spilling various mutilations of rock music into the milling crowds, but after a couple of blocks I was stopped by a clot of tee shirt shoppers. A woman who could have posed as a Norman Rockwell grandmother had selected *I wasn't born a bitch – men like you made me this way* and a boy with a high school complexion was trying to decide between *Wanted: a meaningful overnight relationship* and *Smile – it's the second best thing you can do with your mouth.*

To get past the shoppers I circled into the street, where I was blocked by two men climbing into one of the bicycle rickshaws that serve as Key West taxicabs. I noticed the conch tattoo first, and when I looked into the doll face of the other man our eyes locked. Arthur the dealer. The small permanent smile didn't flicker, but the pale eyes widened.

On an impulse to somehow exploit his surprise I took a step to block their way and, as Arthur settled into the seat, I said, "Hey, I've been hoping I'd run into you. I've been looking for a little action, and I thought you might know where there's a worthwhile game."

Arthur cocked his head, as if studying my face, and then he leaned forward so that I could hear him answer just above a whisper: "You'd better get out of the way of my vehicle. People who get in the way get hurt."

Startled, I stepped back and they pedaled away. I glanced at the other man again and got a glimpse of a gray ponytail and a confirming look at the pink-lipped tattoo I'd seen at Armond's party. In my mind's ear I could hear Armond say, "Remember, pot limit," which Harry had thought meant "nothing harder than marijuana." But Armond had been talking about poker. And those two were probably on their way now to Gisu's "really worth while" pot limit game.

I decided the beach was the only place to jog and went back to the condo. To stop speculating about what might have happened in pot limit poker – or what Armond might have gotten in the way of – to land him in his pool, I sorted through the shelf of paperbacks that the tenants used as a trading library, found a *Pirates of the Spanish Main* and finally got to sleep over the Piet Heyn's capture of the 1629 treasure fleet.

A siren wailed its way through a confused and unsettling dream and finally woke me, sweaty and certain that something awful was happening. I stared at the ceiling, thinking, if the phone rings to notify me that Gregg is sick or in trouble I'll never doubt ESP. Then it occurred to me that no one could call me about Gregg because only Harry knew where I was. I had an impulse to call Gregg, just to make sure he was all right, but of course it was the middle of the night there, too. What would I say – I heard a siren here in Key West and got worried about you? You see, son, when you're all alone without a hell of a lot to look forward to, you wake up with strange notions.

I woke late. Last night's premonition was clinging to me, but in the raw subtropical sunshine on the roof terrace where I took my coffee it seemed incredible that I had actually considered calling Gregg in the middle of the night because a street noise had wakened me. Exercise, I decided. Punish the body and clear the head.

Looking over the parapet I could see the tourists already

clogging Duval. Only place to jog was the beach. I wondered when the tide would be low. Whenever, the odds were twelve to one against meeting her at any given time. But I still didn't want to take the chance, and so I settled for some calisthenics here on the roof.

I'd finished my stretches and pushups and was punishing my abs with sit-ups when the phone rescued me: "Get you out of the shower?" Marge asked. "You sound out of breath." And then, before I could think of a bright answer: "Got a date for lunch?"

"No – can I pick you up?"

"No, but you could meet me at El Poco Loco."

"Where's that?"

"In Little Cuba, on Catharine Street. Around twelve-thirty?"

After I hung up I located Catharine on my tourist map. Unknown territory to me, and so I pedaled down there a few minutes early, past the Frederick Douglas Community Center where a bronze and black rooster strutted across the street with territorial arrogance, to find what turned out to be a tiny mom-and-pop advertising "commida Hispana" and furnished with straight-back wooden chairs, scarred tables and a garlic ambience. I took a table against the wall, where I could see her arrive, beyond two Spanish-speaking families who were digging into black beans, yellow rice and fried plantains. Before I finished a cup of coffee she was at the door.

For a moment I thought she was someone else. Her cap-cut brown hair was hidden under a floppy hat patterned with camouflage splotches. Goggle-eyed sunglasses concealed half her face, and instead of the put-together look I'd come to expect she was wearing baggy cargo pants and an oversize man's shirt with the sleeves rolled half way to the elbows. She glanced behind her as she came in, took off her glasses and nodded when she saw me stand up.

"Now, *this* is a kitchen where the boss looks at every plate before it's served," she said after she'd hung the shapeless hat on a wall hook and taken the chair across from me. "Try the ropa vieja – best this side of Havana. And the key lime pie is always slightly tart with a meringue that's just tanned."

As we ordered she continued the bright chatter that seemed as uncharacteristic as her sloppy clothes. When the waiter had taken our orders I said, "What's going on, Marge?"

She looked away and bit her lip. "They–" she began, cleared her throat and started again: *"Bottom Line* – she was torched last night."

I must have looked like I'd been kicked in the stomach because she reached across the table and squeezed my hand. After a while I managed to ask, "When?"

"Must have been three, maybe three-thirty in the morning. Phone woke me." When I clenched my fist she leaned back and slid her hands up under the half-way sleeves, and hugging her elbows. "He was talking through some – I don't know – a tin can maybe. Made him sound spooky. You know, when you just wake up? Like a nightmare."

"What did he say?"

She shook her head. "Don't remember exactly. Something like, this is a message for you and your boy friend, and you can't prove anything. After he hung up I was trying to write it down. You know, so I'd remember – and then I heard sirens."

I remembered. "Woke me up too. I thought – never mind. Go on."

"When I went out on my balcony I could see it. Josh used to sit out there and just look at that boat. 'Second prettiest thing in my life,' he'd say. That was back in the good times." She flashed a rueful smile. "Anyway, I know just where our mooring is. And the fire was so bright I could see all over the harbor. I stood out there a long time." She looked away and bit her lip again. "Watching her burn."

"Key West have fire boats?" I asked.

"I never saw one. But *Bottom Line* never sank. Just burned down to the water and sizzled out. Brave little boat."

Our lunch came. I picked at the shredded beef and put my fork down. "Marge, I–"

She held up her hand to stop me. "I didn't bring you here for apologizing and second-guessing. I got myself into this, remember? I'm here to deliver the part of the message that was for you."

I tried some of the plantain, but it stuck in my throat. After half a glass of water I managed: "They don't know who I am, but they called you at home."

She smiled, her eyes still brimming. "Everyone at the marina knows our boat."

"Stupid of me," I said. "Hanging a towel over the stern so they couldn't read the name. I should have–" I couldn't think of what I should have done, and what I shouldn't have done was sufficiently obvious that I started over: "What have you told the police?"

"Not much. He was right – what proof do I have? Wouldn't do any good, and maybe it's not smart."

I thought about that. "Police might question them anyway. You know, go around to all the boats. Especially now, when they're investigating a murder."

Her eyes widened. "I hadn't thought of that."

"If the cops question them, they'll suppose–"

She nodded. "I know."

"Marge, if they got your phone number they can get your address."

She pulled a face as if tasting something sour. "I've moved out. For the time being."

I was thinking, God, what have I gotten you into? But all I said was, "You have – some place safe?"

"A friend. I'm fine, Burke."

"For the moment," I said.

She smiled, biting her lip at the same time. "Hey, that's where we live, isn't it? In the moment?"

We both tried to deal with some of the beans and rice. After a while I said, "You're right, *Bottom Line* was a brave boat. She behaved herself nicely in that squall. What are you going to tell Josh?"

Keeping her head down Marge said, "I'm going to tell him, that's what insurance is for. I'm *not* going to tell him that we're probably both better off without that boat. But I think we are. I know I am."

I went back to the ropa vieja. After a while Marge looked up and explained: "Who needs to be reminded of a failed marriage all the time? I packed the snapshots away years ago. Marina's going to tow what's left of *Bottom Line* off the mooring tomorrow and then, every time I walk out onto the balcony I won't think of–" she shrugged a self-deprecating gesture "– young love. I'll bet you don't keep anything around. No lonely letters or anniversary gifts, do you?"

I gave up on lunch. "No, but I've lived a lot of my life out of a sea chest. Makes it easy to leave sentimental things behind." She sat back also, and I signaled for coffee. "You know," I forced a smile, "sentimental things, like family, and responsibilities."

"Starting to catch up with you?" she said, trying to lighten the moment.

"What's catching up with me–" I began, and then waited

while the bus boy cleared our table. "On a clear day," I started over, "I can see that what I just said was a cop-out. You know, the occupational hazard thing. Things didn't fall apart at home because of the Navy. That's a cop-out." And then, to change the subject: "This friend you're staying with – nobody can find you there?"

"I'm being very careful." She pulled the big sunglasses out of her shirt pocket and held them against her face, mugging a sober look. "Never go out without my disguise."

We shared a smile, and then she said: "About the cop-out, you don't need to beat up on yourself all the time. That's unproductive, too."

"I do feel guilty," I said. "Now I've got you hiding out, and your boat – tell me, how do *you* feel about it?"

"Truthfully?" She leaned forward. "I'm so *fucking* mad I could bite nails." I must have flinched at the uncharacteristic obscenity because she leaned back with her head cocked, observing me, as she added, "Which is also unproductive, of course."

She stood up, put on the hat and cocked the sunglasses on the brim. "I'm not going to give you my friend's number, but I'll call home a couple of times a day to get the messages off my machine. I'm a little paranoid today, so if you don't mind, I'd rather we didn't leave together."

"Only the paranoid survive," I said. "That's Duval tee shirt wisdom."

"And the guy who called me – you got the message, right? I mean, you didn't just hear it, you've taken it on board."

"Message is stowed on board," I said. "And I'm fucking mad too."

"Not mad enough to do something stupid." She made it a statement but waited for an answer.

102

"I've already been stupid enough for the whole year. How long do you..." I trailed off, not knowing how to ask the question.

"How long am I going to be hiding out?" She pulled the glasses down. "I don't know. How long are you going to be in the treasure hunting business?"

"That's what got–" I backed up and started over: "What if I go to the police?"

"And tell them what?"

"About the dive site and the boat chase."

"What's the difference – you tell them or I tell them?"

I thought about that. "Can I call and talk to your machine?"

"Might be better if you didn't."

I realized what she was telling me, but I didn't want to accept it. "I understand," I said, "but at night I'll look for a green light on the end of your dock."

She stared at me through the owlish glasses. "You remember *Gatsby*?"

"Reading it now. Trying to impress you."

She turned, threaded through the tables and went out without looking back. Watching her leave in those shapeless cargo pants I thought of the bunch-and-release of buttocks under the wet cotton shorts as I had boosted her up onto the stern of the boat. At the door she looked up and down the street, ready to confront at eye level whatever was there, and as I watched her stride out of sight I found my fists balled in my lap and my eyes filling.

I gave her ten minutes of separation time, which was long enough for the soup of emotions she'd left to congeal into an indigestible wad of anger, and then I paid the check and unhooked the bike from the rack on the sidewalk. I pedaled over to the Jolly Roger office so oblivious to everything around me that I almost ran over a zonked-out girl, not much older than Gregg, who was wandering across Simonton Street.

Today, a skinny young man wearing a wispy brown beard and a Jolly Roger tee shirt was at the reception desk. When I asked to see Roger he said, "Sorry, but he's aboard the barge."

"Be back this afternoon?"

He shook his head. "I doubt it. Sea trials next week. But he'll call in for his messages." He offered me a memo pad.

As I wrote my name and the condo phone number I said, "Tell him I have a report on the doubloon assignment." I wrote "doubloon" on the pad under my name and number. "Unless I hear from him I'll be here at ten tomorrow morning. And he really needs to hear what I have to tell him."

"Can't promise anything," he said. "Getting ready for sea – they're all working twenty hour days."

"Just tell him." And then, on my way out: "You have a local tide table?"

He did, and I found that low was at 7:08 PM – over three hours from now. As I started pedaling down to the harbor I remembered the telescope on Harry's roof terrace and turned around to go back to the condo.

I built a pot of watch-standers' coffee, starting at double strength and improving with time on the warming plate, and carried a mug onto the terrace. I got the telescope focused, found the blackened ruin of *Bottom Line* and could even make out wisps of still-rising smoke. Beyond that hulk a man in a skiff tossed a net for bait in the shallows, which reminded me of the man on the jetty the first day I saw Gisu, and the Tuscan frieze of the gladiator with his net and trident.

Farther out, near the harbor entrance, I located what must be *Happy Daze*. Then I examined every sport fisherman in the harbor, even those alongside the pier waiting for charters, but none had the gin pole that would identify *Dutch Treat.*

Arson last night, back out on the dive site today. Work ethic. Treasure psychosis, Roger would say. Target fixation, Harry would say.

I poured another mug and thought about that. I remembered Harry coming into my stateroom after our first mission and announcing, "You scared me shitless."

"Me too," I admitted. "Just now my knees got wobbly."

"You know what the problem is?"

"Sure. Target fixation."

"Say it again," Harry said.

I could hear him now, in what became our pre-strike ritual. Soon after launch, when we were still at a comfortable altitude and "feet wet" with the coastline and our first turning point a few miles ahead, I'd say into the intercom, "Ask me the questions, Harry."

"You know what the problem is?"

"Target fixation."

"Say it again."

Thinking about it now, I said out loud, "My problem is target fixation."

I knew it was now time for me to break off the attack, call the airlines, pack up and turn my key in to Harry's condo manager. I also knew I wasn't going to do that. I tried to understand why. Roger and his treasure hunt? No. I owed Roger a report tomorrow morning, nothing more. Gisu? Something to remember, and to avoid. A score to settle with the guys who'd chased us and then torched *Bottom Line*? Some of that, sure. I was fucking mad. And, I eventually admitted, I wanted to see Marge again.

I went back to the telescope and studied *Happy Daze.* As she swung slightly on the mooring I could see into the cockpit: no magazine, sun glasses, drink can or other sign of habitation. The companionway into the cabin was closed off with hatch boards. Standing in the mid-afternoon sun my shirt was stuck to my back and I knew that, without some circulating air, the boat cabin would be a sauna. Nobody could be aboard. I looked at my watch: still four hours before low tide. I wondered if Gisu was in some other rented room, showing some other guy what she really, really wanted.

I went inside and called Harry's office, expecting to leave a message with his secretary. Instead, she put him on and he opened with, "You find some bonefish?"

"Haven't gotten out on the flats. Weather's been squally."

"Been off shore?"

"Once. Actually, twice," I dissembled uncomfortably. "Caught some big jacks one day, but the next time a line squall chased us in. Is it time for me to turn this pad over to a paying guest?"

"Apparently not."

"Apparently?"

"Told the manager to let me know if somebody wants the penthouse, and I haven't heard from him. Haven't heard anything about Paul either. Cop called and talked to me on the phone once, that's all."

"Talked to me once too," I said. "Haven't seen anything in the paper after the first day."

"Hope they find whoever it was. I liked Paul. But I don't know how you investigate a crime in a city that turns over half its population every week. You keeping out of trouble without me to look after you?"

"I decided to go ahead and answer that ad. The Jolly Roger."

"And you've been out treasure hunting?"

"They're still outfitting the barge. Getting ready for sea

trials. I also talked to your friend Marge – about what it would take to get her back into the business."

"That's a possibility?"

"She said to tell you that it's impossible. But then she gave me sort of an answer."

"What sort of an answer?"

"She'd have to own fifty-one per cent and she'd serve no ranch dressing."

Harry laughed over the phone. "Sounds like you've entered negotiations. You seeing a lot of this lady?"

"Also, she'll serve no strip sirloin. Everything has to be fresh that day, and she has to look at every dish coming out of the kitchen."

"How can she do that?"

"That's what she said – it's impossible."

"Burke, if by any chance you happen to see her again, you tell Marge that I accept all her conditions. Impossible or not. Now I gotta go – enjoy the condo, and happy negotiations."

I poured another cup and decided to try Gregg again. This time he answered his private line: "Lo?"

"Hey, glad to catch you out of that computer game land."

"Hi dad."

"How're things going, son?"

"Fine."

"How's school?"

"Okay."

"Going out for football this year?"

"I don't know. Maybe. Takes a lotta time."

I suppressed the impulse to say, "Time away from computer quest game?" and substituted: "How're the grades?"

"Okay. Look dad, I'm studying for a math test now, okay?"

"Sure, son. I'm down at Key West now, and I was thinking

– maybe you'd like to try bone fishing with me some time."

"Sure."

"Okay, I'll talk to your mom about it. Good luck on the test."

"Thanks. G'bye."

I hung up, feeling farther away from him than before I'd called. If I could arrange a fishing trip, I wondered what we'd talk about. Transitions, maybe. Adolescence is the most perilous of all. What would I advise him? Something about facing issues when they come up. Try to explain that the longer you put off any part of growing up, the harder it is to get it done. Maybe something about learning to chart your own course. You don't want to go out for football? Fine. And if you do go out, it's because you want to play the game, not because somebody expects you to or because it could help you get into Annapolis. But mostly we'd talk about all the different kinds of fish and how each one works out its own way to make a living. Fishing is about understanding all that. Maybe I'd take him snorkeling. He could see some spectacular transitions out on the reef.

Which made me realize that I hadn't been in the water myself this trip. My scuba gear was piled in Harry's hall closet; maybe I could get a place on a dive boat after I talked to Roger tomorrow. In the meantime I changed into swim trunks, took the mask and snorkel tube and pedaled down to the Casa Marina pier. The water was stinging cold at first and clearer than I expected. I drifted through the buoyant inner space among shifting schools of sergeant majors, grunts and snappers, emptying my mind. Near the end of the pier I thought I saw three snook, unusual this far south, and farther out a barracuda hung motionless near the surface, watching me with a frozen leer. When I climbed onto the bicycle again I felt refreshed, loosened and back in charge of my own life.

I didn't want to see Gisu again, but with Marge at risk I had to do something, and Gisu was my only connection to the treasure hunt. I decided to wait for her at low tide and then play the scene by ear.

Pedaling toward Fort Zach beach, I didn't see the white Mercury until it was alongside, idling along at bicycle speed with Scully beaming his upperclassman's sneer out the passenger side window. I managed to ignore them for perhaps half a block but finally said, "Something I can do for you, officer?"

"Take care of yourself" Scully said, "out there in the water."

"You were watching me? When I was snorkeling?"

"Wouldn't do for you to get shark bit or something. You're involved in a murder investigation, you know."

"Involved? Because I was at a party with dozens of other people?"

"You just be careful. We'll be keeping an eye on you." As Morales moved the car ahead, releasing traffic accumulated behind them, Scully turned around in his seat to watch me out of sight.

I got to the beach a little after six thirty. As I stretched my hamstrings I watched the trade wind out of the northeast ruffling cat's paws beyond the jetty. A couple of families were at the picnic tables under the pines, but except for three kids throwing a frisbee the beach was empty. By the time I had jogged my two miles and walked back to the bike the tide was dead low, but Gisu had not appeared.

I waited until after dark and then pedaled back to the condo, stopping at the Chinese restaurant for take-out and the video store for a rental movie. While the sweet and sour soup was in the microwave I went back to the telescope on the terrace. *Happy Daze* was dark and deserted.

I called and left a message on Marge's machine: "Harry accepts the fifty-one per cent and ranch dressing and all the other conditions. I told him it's still impossible. Have you ever fished permit and bonefish? It's like hunting, except that you catch and release. Good night for now."

Before I started the movie I put the telescope again on the shapeless shadow that was *Happy Daze*. I could imagine Joey Doubles and Dutch anchored on the treasure site, waiting to dive at first light, but where was Gisu?

CHAPTER 7
Homophobic Rage

"Nobody out there," Roger said, waving a gesture toward the chart on the wall behind him. "Billy flew all four grids – nothing. Off to the west there was a charter boat trolling. Billy flew down low enough to see the wakes of the birds off the outriggers. Just four fishermen."

"I don't understand," I said. "One day it's a big enough deal – whatever it is out there– to chase us and then torch the boat, and the next day they're gone. Could they have grabbed the treasure and run?"

Roger shook his head. "It's not sitting down there in a pile. Remember, we're talking four hundred years. Storms with thirty, fifty foot seas. Anything down there is scattered around, and covered with sand. They might have to dive for weeks just to know what they'd found."

"I can't believe they just gave up," I said. "Could they have gone someplace for more equipment?"

Roger nodded slowly as he thought about that, and then he stood up and ran a thick finger along one of the gridlines on the chart behind his desk. "Looks like forty to sixty feet out there. Deeper in places. Plenty of visibility after the murk from the squall settles, but they'd need a good diver to search for anything small."

"He doesn't have any experience under water," I said. "Joey Doubles doesn't. Guys at the marina said he took the scuba class – you know, what the dive boat people give the tourists – took it just a couple of weeks ago. And the *Dutch Treat* guy – they call him a boat gypsy. He's probably never done any serious diving."

Roger took his seat again. "That could be it. Maybe it's too much for them. Too deep. Especially in this squally weather when it's hard just to hold an anchor position. And the bottom might be broken, hard to see anything small."

"So what would they do?"

"If they're smart, they'd do what I'm doing. Use this season for outfitting and sea trials and start search and recovery in a couple of weeks. High pressure weather ought to sit down on us, then, for a few days at a time."

"That's if they're smart," I pressed. "What if they've got a bad case of treasure psychosis and all they can think about is, somebody knows. Knows where they're diving."

He pursed his lips and looked off at some vanishing point over my head. "He tried to hire me – contract for one of my divers, remember? Maybe they're looking for someone who can work at that depth."

"And cut someone else in on the treasure?"

He raised one palm in an ambiguous gesture. "Maybe not. If they kept the hired hand below decks until they got out of sight of land and then didn't give him the GPS numbers, how'd he know where he was?"

"So where would they go?"

"Not far. Not if they're traveling by boat. They'd want to be in a reasonable distance from the site. Probably some place with a dive shop."

I followed his logic: "Where they might hire a diver."

"Also supplies. They could get fuel and water at any marina, but to recharge their air they'd need a dive shop."

"So where is the nearest dive shop up island?"

He stood and went to the chart on the wall. "Nearest one is just across the causeway on Stock Island," he said. "Too close." He pointed to one of the string of islands curling toward the tip of Florida. "He'd probably run up to Big Pine Key. About forty miles from here, but less than that from their dive site."

"Why don't you send Billy up there. Look for a gin pole."

Roger pulled a rueful expression. "I'll try. See if Billy can work me in between all the Miami jobs he's getting."

"Suppose they're up there, in Big Pine. Then what do you do?"

"Get our sea trials done as quick as we can. Get out there in that grid. Try to locate what they think they have."

"What if they're already on it?"

"They'll have to stay on it. Until a court says it's theirs, they can't leave it without losing their claim."

"What court has jurisdiction out there?" I asked.

"That's a little ambiguous. In one case a federal district court assumed jurisdiction. But they'd need an admiralty lawyer, and time to file papers."

"Not their style. If they're up in Big Pine, I'll bet they're trying to get down on the wreck and grab as much as they can."

Roger nodded. "Probably ruin the artifacts and scatter more than they recover."

"Maybe I'll just drive up there and have a look around."

"What's the point? Say you find them, then what?"

"Then at least we'd know."

"Know what?"

"Know that they're still working the site. Haven't given it up."

"Either way, as soon as we've got the barge operational I'm going to search that area." Roger leaned toward me. "You're not going up there because you're pissed off about your friend's boat, are you?" When I didn't answer he went on: "Because there's nothing you can do about that. Nothing useful."

I stood up. "I guess you're right. Am I in your log for a little piece of anything you find on the numbers I gave you?"

He stood and offered his hand. "We find anything, I'll be in touch."

As I pedaled back to the condo I already knew I was going to Big Pine, and in my typical backward planning process I tried to work out a rationale. Who knows what I might find? Gisu and Joey Doubles – that team wasn't going to last much longer. And Dutch didn't make it any more stable. Especially not with a little treasure psychosis in the mix. And now that I'd created a situation where Marge's boat was destroyed and she was hiding out, well, I couldn't just walk away from that. For that matter, I couldn't just walk away from her.

This time I saw Morales and Scully getting out of their Mercury in front of the moped rental shop. I snapped the lock on the bicycle and waited for them to cross over to the sidewalk.

Morales, in a different combination of what seemed like the same earth-tones, held out his hand. "Hello, Mr. Bascomb. How is the fishing?" Scully hung back without the sneer, letting the good cop make polite inquiry.

"Got caught in that squall the other day," I said. "How has *your* fishing been? Any leads on the Armond case?"

He shrugged an ambiguous gesture. "Maybe. We were hoping you might be able to help us."

"Told you everything I remember."

"I know you did. But maybe, if you saw someone who was at the party – Mr. Armond's party – maybe you'd recognize him?"

"You mean, in some kind of a line-up?"

The two of them exchanged a smile. "No, no – nothing like that." He took my elbow and gently turned me toward the street. "Just come with us for beer, look around the bar and see if anyone looks familiar – okay?"

I pulled my arm back and stopped at the curb. "Why me? I told you – I didn't know any of those people."

"That's exactly why. If you recognize someone, there's a good chance he was at the party, right?"

There was something wrong with that logic, but before I could frame a demur Scully said, "You *do* want to help us solve that crime, don't you, Mr. Bascomb?"

I looked at him, trying to read the expressionless eyes over the slight downward curl of his mouth, but Morales urged: "It'll just take a few minutes. Drink a beer, look around, see if you recognize anyone? Be a big help to us."

I looked at my watch, as if I were dealing with a busy schedule, said "Okay, sure" and they fell into step on either side of me. At the car Scully took the driver's seat and Morales insisted I take the front passenger place.

"Where we going?" I asked.

"Couple blocks," Scully said. "Place called the Lavender Goose. Know it?"

"No. What kind of a place is it?"

"Just a bar. Local hang-out." When he pulled into a blue-lined "handicapped" parking place in front of Eckerd Drug Store we got out and walked next door, under a cartoon goose outlined in neon that probably glowed lavender at night, and into air conditioned gloom.

An L-shaped bar filled half the deep, narrow room. As we found our way to a booth near the elbow of the bar I noticed that the mutter of ambient conversation seemed to pause and then slowly restart. When my eyes began to adjust I made out four young men playing dollar bill poker on the bar and half a dozen others in twos and threes among the other booths. A stringy youngster with spiky bleached hair and a row of studs in his left ear took our orders: draft Sam Adams for me and coffee for the others.

"See anybody you know?" asked Scully.

I looked around. "Nobody I recognize," I said.

"Sure?" said Morales.

I was conscious of the two of them watching me as I tried to scan the room unobtrusively. And then the obvious dawned. "This is a gay bar," I said.

"Of course," Scully said. "This is a Key West bar. Queers make you uncomfortable?"

"A little," I admitted. "Feel out of place, I suppose."

"You must have encountered homosexuals in the Navy," Morales said.

"Sure."

"Any ever come on to you?" asked Scully.

"You didn't bring me here to see if I could recognize anyone, did you?" I said.

Scully curled that smile into an arc. "Hey, I know how you feel," he said. "They make my flesh crawl too."

"I didn't say that."

Scully leaned toward me, elbows on the table. "I'll bet no fag every came onto you the second time, right? Bet you punched his lights out."

I drank some beer and then looked from Scully to Morales. "Where is this going, officers?"

Morales answered: "Mr. Bascomb, would you be willing to take a voluntary lie detector test?"

"About what?"

"About what happened the night of Mr. Armond's party?"

I sat back and took a deep breath. "What did I tell you about that night that you don't believe?"

Morales raised one hand in a placating gesture. "This is just for confirmation?" He phrased it as a question, as if asking me to understand. "Just so we can cross you off our list?"

"Your list of suspects?"

He shrugged. "This is a murder investigation. We have to be very thorough?"

"Why should I volunteer for a lie detector test?"

Scully answered. "Because you have nothing to worry about. Because you've been telling us the truth all along, and that will prove it."

"I don't think I have to prove anything to you, officer." I took a moment to assemble what I was going to say next. "But I think *you* need to tell *me* why you lured me into a place like this for questioning."

Scully nodded, as if "now we're getting somewhere" and glanced at Morales. "Queers really get you upset, don't they Bascomb? Make you defensive. Fight or flight, right?"

"No."

Morales put in: "Would you tell us how you feel about homosexuals, Mr. Bascomb?"

"Sure. And then you'll tell me why you brought me here?"

Morales nodded. "Of course."

I looked around the bar. The dollar bill poker game had broken up and the players had been absorbed into one of the groups around a booth in the back. Nothing about the appearance or behavior of any of the men sent a signal. I turned back to Morales, trying to ignore Scully. "I think it's probably complicated. Homosexuality. I've known a couple of guys that I think were probably born cross-wired, and others that didn't care what they stuck their dicks into. Maybe they're not even homosexuals – they just commit homosexual acts. And then I've known some others that I think may have been turned. You know, influenced, when they were still young and trying to figure themselves out."

117

"By an older man?" Morales asked.

When I nodded, he leaned slightly forward. "You think homosexuals are predatory?"

"Some are, sure. So are some straights."

Scully said, "And the predatory ones – what do you think should happen to them?"

Now I looked at him. "I don't know. It's complicated, like I said." I turned back to Morales: "I think I've answered your question. Now are you going to answer mine?"

He shrugged a little accommodating gesture. "We're exploring an idea. Trying a hypothesis?"

When I nodded that I understood he went on: "You see, Mr. Armond was not just drowned. He was badly beaten first. Probably with a little statue from the garden. The kind of thing they carve in the islands. It's supposed to look like–" he searched for the word "–a god? An idol? It has a penis as big as its leg."

A chorus of laughter from the booth at back of the bar caused us to glance in that direction, and when I looked back I noticed that Scully was watching my reaction. Morales went on: "He wasn't just beaten. He was also mutilated." And then, after a moment to give me time to react, "His penis was cut off." Another pause. "And stuffed in his mouth."

My fists clenched involuntarily. To recover, I drank off the rest of my beer before I said, "So what's that got to do with me?"

Morales said, "That kind of mutilation, that's a signature. A sign post. It says, 'homophobic rage'."

I looked from one to the other. The waiter came and I put my hand over my glass to signal no more. Morales looked around the room, but Scully never took his eyes off me. "Nice place, don't you think?" he said with a smug little smile that tried to suggest a shared understanding.

"So that's why you brought me here?" I said. "To watch me react to homosexuals?"

"All you have to do," Scully said, "is agree to take that test."

Now I was the one who leaned into him. "Wrong. All I have to do is get up and walk out of here. The way Harry and I walked out of that party early. People must have seen us."

He leaned forward too, protecting his space. "But you went back, didn't you? After everybody had left, except those two sweet young things up in the bedroom who were only paying attention to each other. What did Armond say that made you go back? He make a pass at you?"

I looked back at Morales, remembering. "You asked me about this before – how I feel about homosexuals. Why me? Because I was in the Navy?"

He shrugged. "It *has* been a problem for the Navy, wouldn't you agree?" I decided not to answer that, and he went on: "We believe we now know who was at the party. Talked to most of them. They're all Key West people. Comfortable with homosexuals. You're the only off-islander, and so we have to wonder about you."

I stood and slid out of the booth. "I'll leave you conchs here in your–" I took a deep breath, selecting my words "– comfortable lavender ambience. And I'll cool off walking back to the condo."

Scully moved, as if to stand up, and I said to him, "It's not homos that piss me off. It's bureaucrats, politicians, cops – people who abuse their little authority."

I left five dollars on the table, saying, "Don't put my beer on your expense account," and went out, hesitating a moment in the sudden glare. As I walked, I tried to remember the people I'd seen at Armond's, wondering whether I really had been the only off-islander. I remembered the porno conch tattoo guy that I'd seen later with Arthur, and the couple warming up next to the bird cage and the guys in the muscle shirts. They'd all seemed to be regular parts of the Key West after-dark scene, along with the two girls that laughed in harmony at our table and their two older guys. Marge had seemed to know them.

One of them had said something about "Joe weed trouble."

I had supposed "Joe weed" was a local term for marijuana, but I hadn't been paying attention because I was listening to Marge. Sounding the words in my head now, "Joe weed trouble," I stopped in mid-stride. Joeweedouble. Joey Doubles. They'd been talking about the Doublooner.

I turned and started back to the Lavender Goose to tell Morales that I might not have been the only off-islander at the party that night. But I'd have to tell Scully at the same time, and I had nothing to say to him. I stopped, hesitating. Then I remembered: if they questioned the Doublooner, he'd suppose that Marge had fingered him. I went on to the condo.

CHAPTER 8
Buenas Tarde Señor Galeón

As I drove A1A North – which, with typical Key West disregard of the rules, runs east – across the string of arching bridges that lace islands to the mainland, I listened to tapes I'd checked out of the Key West public library, using Harry's card, of *Sir Henry Morgan's Adventures on the Spanish Main*. A hundred years of war down here, sacking cities and sinking ships. Treasure psychosis.

At Stock Island I parked in front of the sign above a cement block building that advertised charters, rentals and dive trips. Inside was an efficient display of fishing and diving gear with no one to make a sale or stop a shoplifter. I walked through the back door to a dock.

Tanks of live shrimp and what looked like spearing along the back wall were sustained by a continuous spray pumped from the harbor. Fifteen-foot boats, with hundred-and-fifty horse engines and poling platforms for fishing eight-inch water on the flats, were tied to the pier. I watched torpedo shadows of tarpon drifting in the lagoon until a bony young man wearing more tattoos than clothes came around the end of the building carrying a limber graphite pole.

I asked some questions about the fishing – permit were tailing this morning – and then asked if he'd seen a boat called *Dutch Treat*. As I expected, he hadn't, and so I went back to the Toyota baking in the lot.

Heading east on AIA North, the air conditioner made too much noise catching up with the morning heat for me to listen to Henry Morgan for a while. I decided that, at this stage of a mission I needed to talk. Lacking Harry, in the whirring throughway cocoon I replied – occasionally out loud – to what I knew damn well Harry would say.

So maybe this doesn't make a hell of a lot of sense. Okay, so what? Missions never make sense. When did we ever fly a mission that made sense? If they made sense they wouldn't be missions. They'd be, I don't know, enterprises. Something like that. Missions are what you have to do. Roger needs to know if those people are in Big Pine, so that's an objective. Not a very good one, but an objective. But – now get this, Harry – the next place that can recharge tanks is too far up island. Too far to get back and forth to their dive site. Which means, Harry, if they're not in Big Pine, then they're outta here. Gone, presumably with a load of treasure that none of them wants to be separated from. Why else would they leave *Happy Daze* behind? Which would mean Marge could breathe easy. Maybe she can't go home, just yet. Not while *Happy Daze* is still waiting out there. Actually, Gisu and Joey might decide to buy any future boat they need in some anonymous island marina rather than come back to Key West, where people might remember them. But if *Dutch Treat* is gone, at least Marge wouldn't be looking up and down the street every day, thinking of me as the guy who brought paranoia into her life. Hell of a fine objective, Harry. So, when we look at it that way, this mission makes perfect sense.

And yes, I will beware of target fixation. All I have to do is find the dive shop, look around, spot the *Dutch Treat,* or not spot her. Either way, mission accomplished.

It so, then why, you ask, did I throw my scuba gear in the trunk, along with my clean clothes from the Laundromat? Well, if I tell Roger that *Dutch Treat*'s not in sight in the harbor, he's going to ask how I know they weren't out on the site, don't you think? Which means I might to have to strike up a conversation with the guys at the dive shop to find out if they've seen anything of *Dutch Treat*. I've found that getting information from these conchs is no cinch, so I'd better look like a customer, with gear in hand.

But it turned out to be easier than that.

I didn't stop at Boca Chica because I'd flown into the air station there and I knew there was no dive shop on the island. Sugarloaf Key was just a pause for gasoline and a trip to the head, and the next island was Big Pine Key.

Another strip mall with bar-restaurant, a 7-ll, a souvenir shop, a bank and some other stores that I ignored when I saw another cement-block building under a sign announcing game fishing, diving and glass-bottom boat trips. The oyster-shell parking lot was empty, but when I walked around the end of the building – there, in the harbor, swinging gently on a mooring, was the bad news. I couldn't see the name on her transom, but the gin pole on the port side of the cockpit was unmistakable. Good news for Roger. All I had to do now was turn around, drive back and report that the hunt was still on. But what would I say to Marge?

As if to give me a clue, someone came through the companionway into the cockpit of *Dutch Treat*. I hadn't brought binoculars – stupid – and so I couldn't make out a black straight-edge moustache, but even from here I could see that this wasn't Gisu. He climbed out onto the foredeck, checked the mooring line and the hatch dogs, edged back to the cockpit and pulled a line to haul an inflatable boat into my field of view. Was it the same boat Gisu had rowed back to *Happy Daze* that night after the casino cruise?

I watched him load a scuba cylinder into the inflatable, uncleat the painter, climb down the ladder and shove off. As he rowed ashore I studied *Dutch Treat*. No sign of anyone else aboard. If Gisu wasn't aboard either *Dutch Treat* or *Happy*

Daze, where was she?

After the inflatable was out of sight behind the dock house, I walked out on the dock and through a door marked "office." An over-tanned blond, spilling out of the top of a crimson swimsuit, was laughing into a phone behind the counter. I looked around at the snorkel tubes, masks, fins, nose clamps and other scuba miscellany displayed for sale, picked up a leaflet with dive schedules and prices and started back to the door when she said, "Help you?"

I held up the leaflet. "All I need, thanks," and went out.

Next to the office was a long shed with a webwire door padlocked to a stanchion. Inside, hanging from dowel pins, were wet suits, masks, fins and other gear for the rental customers. Beyond that, a dark-skinned youth with loose, swimmer's muscles and wearing a black swimsuit cut like jockey shorts was charging a tank at a noisy compressor. Alongside the pier was a dive boat that I estimated at forty feet, all cockpit with just a fiberglass shelter forward, a pair of benches along the centerline and air bottle racks lining both gunwales.

As I walked out the pier I could see the guy from *Dutch Treat* at the end, exhaling a stream of smoke into the sea breeze. I took in the streaky blond hair, stretched-out tee shirt, unpressed khakis and salted topsiders. Without any clear plan in mind, I asked, "water still murky this morning?"

He glanced around, showing a two-day stubble and a sunglasses tan. "Beginning to clear up," he said. I noticed that I had to look up slightly to meet his delft blue eyes.

"That squall, couple of days ago," I said, "sure roiled up the bottom."

He nodded, took another drag on his cigarette and drifted the smoke out of his thick nose.

Still improvising, I said, "Notice you were out by yourself."

He nodded, looking down, now, at the bait swarming around the piling.

"I get bored with the dive boats myself," I blundered on. "I mean, how many parrot fish do you want to see in your life?"

He shrugged.

He was obviously going to offer nothing, and so I just flat-out asked, "Know anybody diving wrecks around here?"

Now I got the full delft gaze. "What kind of wrecks?"

"Whatever. I've signed on with the Jolly Roger. You know, in Key West?" He nodded, and I kept winging it: "We're going out next week, and so I was thinking about a couple of practice dives, first. You know, get a feel for the conditions."

"You dived a lot of wrecks?"

Now I adopted a dismissive shrug. "A few."

"Around here?" I had his attention.

"Never this far south." Just in case he was thinking about the boat they had chased I said, "Day before yesterday I dived the *San Miguel* off Jupiter. It was murky, they said because you'd had a squall through here."

"How deep is that, Jupiter?"

"Only about fifteen feet. That's why it didn't do much for me."

"Fifteen feet? What was it, a rowboat?"

"Called an Aviso. Like a destroyer, back then. She was supposed to escort the galleons and watch for trouble. This one was carrying contraband."

"Ever dive deeper?"

"Hardly ever that shallow. Where I learned was diving a German sub off Long Island – that's over a hundred. But the conditions are different down here."

He flipped his cigarette at the school of bait and watched

them flash away from the splash and then come back to knock the butt around the surface as they checked to see if it was edible. "You're really a Jolly Roger diver?"

"Got my letter of marque."

"Your what?"

I took it out of my billfold and showed him. "What they call a contract. Treasure hunting bullshit."

He read it through, as if he were getting ready to sign, then re-folded it and handed it back. "You were diving off Jupiter day before yesterday?"

I nodded.

"Date on this contract is over a week ago."

I took my time coming up with an answer, trying for a "what's it to you?" expression. I thought about Jolly Roger's computer sign-in and said, "he's got a web site – that's how I found the job. E-mailed the application and he faxed me what he calls the letter of marque. I'm going to drop by and meet the guy when I get down there tomorrow or the next day."

"You can just show up any time?"

"They're in sea trials now. No work for a diver yet."

He studied me with a guileless blue gaze. "How about this afternoon. Like to go out?"

"You know a wreck site?"

"About forty, fifty feet. You in shape for that?"

"Fifty feet," I said, "that's a tourist dive. More bottom time than air."

"Okay, I'll take you to her."

This was going faster than I expected. Trying to buy some time, I asked, "just fifty feet, it must draw a crowd."

"Not this one," he said, dropping his voice as if someone might be listening. "I found a virgin."

"How old?"

He turned up both palms. "She didn't sink yesterday."

"How do you know?"

He pursed his lips and looked down as if studying a poker hand. Then, turning over a card: "Because coral grows slow."

"There's coral on the wreck?"

Another pause, considering what to disclose. "Not much of a wreck left. That's why nobody's found her. Just some of the metal, and what I could see of that was all crusted up with coral. You got your own gear?"

I gestured back over my shoulder. "In the car."

He looked out over the bay and rasped a knuckle across his stubble, coming to a decision. "Tell you what. I've spent all the time I can afford fooling around down here. Now that I've found that old wreck, well, it's not like there's gold bars and pieces of eight scattered around on top of the sand, y'know what I'm saying? I can see what looks like the ass end of a little cannon and the fluke of an anchor sticking up. But to get the real goodies, what you need is equipment. Something to pump a lot of sand through some kind of a strainer. That the way the Jolly Roger outfit does it?"

"I haven't seen their equipment," I said. "But I know they're fitting out a barge."

He nodded. "That's what you need. A whole boatload of equipment. Now, you're hired on as a diver – if you took them to the spot, put their barge right on top of a treasure ship, I'll bet you'd get a bonus, wouldn't you?"

"I'd sure have a happy boss."

He rasped that cigarette laugh. "You bet you would. Tell you what. I'm not going to get much out of that wreck on my own, y'know what I'm saying? Anyway, right now all I need is enough diesel to get me on my way north. What would you say to three hundred bucks for half day? No check or card."

"Price is fair," I stalled. "How far would we have to run to get out there?"

"Couple hours, maybe less. You'll have plenty of time in the water."

"I don't know if I can–" I back-pedaled, "I wasn't thinking about going out this afternoon."

His thick, sun-bleached brows arched. "Thought you wanted a practice dive. You could practice on the real thing."

"I like that part, but–" I searched for an excuse "–it's just that, this afternoon I don't have three hundred in cash."

"Bank in the mall has an ATM." He looked at his watch. "If we shove off at twelve thirty, you'll have plenty of time." He held out his hand. "My name's Dutch."

"Burke," I said.

"Burke," he repeated, as if sounding it through a memory bank. "Bring whatever you want to drink." He flashed a big customer relations smile.

Ignoring Harry's "target fixation" warning in my head, I asked, "How'd you find it?"

"Guy chartered me to look for it. He knew where to look, all right. But like I say, there's not much of it left, and with the water all roily you'd almost have to bump your nose on it. Anyway, he got discouraged."

"So you went back on your own?"

He grinned and punched my upper arm lightly, as if we were pals. "He thought, old Dutch – he's just a boat bum. My secret is safe with him, y'know what I'm saying?"

"How long did it take you to find it?"

He tilted his head back and rasped a Marlborough man laugh. "We were already on top of it, just about. Next day – first time I went out alone – buenos tarde, Señor Galeón."

"You think it's Spanish?"

He laughed again as we started back down the pier to the dock house. "Ain't some old Cuban fishing boat, that's for sure. That little old cannon, my gin pole would lift it, but I can't keep the sling on it by myself. I need somebody down there to keep the line from drifting off in the tide while I take up the slack. Once it's under tension I think she'll come right up."

He reached out again to touch my arm in a conspiratorial gesture. "That little cannon – I travel light, y'know what I'm saying? We bring it up, you can have it for another couple hundred bucks. Jolly Roger ought to be good for that, don't you think?"

"If it's really old, I think so, sure."

We paused at the railing where his recharged cylinder was waiting. "That cannon," he said, "it looks like it might be bronze. How old would that be?" He climbed down the wooden ladder into the inflatable and I handed the tank to him. I cast off the painter and he cranked the one-lung outboard into life. Puttering away he said, "Twelve thirty this afternoon, partner."

I thought about how old a bronze cannon would be, groping back through what I remembered of military history at the Naval Academy, as I got my tank out of the trunk and left it to be charged. I was pretty sure that John Paul Jones fired cast iron balls out of cast iron guns, and so a bronze piece would be old. Probably old enough to have protected Spanish silver. At the thought I felt a little adrenalin rush, wondering how many Jolly Roger shares I could earn as a finder's fee. It occurred to me that this is how treasure psychosis feels.

Walking off the pier I automatically stopped to check the tide chart posted by the office: high was 9:32 am and 8:14 pm. Driving back to the bank with the ATM I tried to take stock of what I was getting into. The rationalization I'd developed for a surveillance mission – just look around and see if *Dutch Treat* was here – didn't work anymore. But if a three hundred dollar dive charter plus two hundred for an artifact cannon would send Dutch on his way, that was a bargain. Maybe I could keep this palsy relationship going long enough also to find out what happened to Joey Doubles and Gisu. And I might actually bring a Spanish cannon and a treasure site back to Key West.

I knew what Harry would say: "You're going diving with this boat gypsy? Grow up, Burke. You never go up in the air or down under water with someone you can't trust, you know that."

Yes, I did know that. I also knew I was going in spite of knowing better, but at least I could let somebody know where I was and what I was up to. Not that anybody could provide any help out there, but somebody ought to be able to answer the question "I wonder what ever happened to old Burke?"

Who should that be?

Detective Morales? No, he'd have a bunch of questions that I didn't need. Harry? He'd have a lecture that I probably *did* need but didn't want. Marge? At least her machine wouldn't have any back chat. Roger? He'd have to say something about the shares, and I didn't want to negotiate that over the phone. I wanted to just drive up with the bronze cannon in the trunk of my car, walk in and lay the GPS numbers on his desk. Which brought it back to Marge.

I'd noticed a pay phone on the corner in front of the bank and so, after I'd extracted fifteen twenties from the ATM, I called Marge and told her answering machine, "I found Dutch up here in Big Pine Key, and it looks like the beginning of a beautiful friendship. He says Joey Doubles and his lady are long gone, and this afternoon he's going to take me out to the wreck for a fee that'll send him on his way too. I'll call you when we get back in and I've waved him on his way up island. Maybe the next time I see you, I won't have to look into your eyes through those silly sun glasses."

Across the street was an Eckerd. I bought sun block, a six pack of bottled water and a towel, went back to the car, opened the trunk again, threw the wet suit and regulator over my arm and added my swim trunks, mask, fins and bottom-time computer to the Eckerd plastic bag. I left that in a pile on the dock and went back for my dive knife, leaded belt, booties and tank. The youngster with the jockey-shorts swim suit said I could leave my gear in the office while he charged my tank.

On Front Street near the dive shop, the Sea Shanty served me broiled yellowtail and Bass ale while my better judgment argued that I could still get in the car and head back to Key West with mission accomplished. Of course, my better judgment had no chance against target fixation, and so at twelve fifteen I was standing on the dock with my dive gear, watching Dutch row the inflatable in. The first thing he said was, "Find the ATM?" which gave me an idea.

I passed down my gear and bottled water and climbed onto the bow thwart. When Dutch started rowing I said, "Before we slip the mooring, I'd like a little pre-dive conference."

He interrupted his stroke and, with both oar tips out of the water, twisted around to face me. "Conference?"

"Tide will be slack around three thirty. That gives us time to review the bidding. You know, make sure we understand each other."

He dipped the oars again. "What's to understand?" Speaking over his shoulder, he resumed the practiced little dinghy strokes that kept up momentum with minimum effort. "Three hundred for the charter, two hundred for the cannon – that the deal?"

"That's the deal," I said, watching the lats gather and release under his tee shirt. Kept himself in good shape for a boat bum. "I want to give you half the charter up front. You know, earnest money. Make us both more comfortable."

He shook his head. "Not necessary, partner, but if that makes you comfortable, why not?"

He laid the inflatable alongside the ladder and steadied it while I climbed into *Dutch Treat's* cockpit. He handed the gear up to me, climbed into the cockpit and said, with a gesture toward the companionway, "Make yourself at home while I tie up the dink."

I watched him lead the inflatable forward, maneuvering the painter around the gin pole to side-step past the cabin, and I noticed that the gin pole was rigged with what looked like new three-eighths inch nylon leading out of a big coil on the deck. I glanced around the cockpit: fighting chair under a frayed canvas cover, bleached teak deck with a cast net bunched sloppily in one of the scuppers, bait knife in one of the rod holders and a five-foot gaff in another. A bungee cord stretched from fuel tank cap to one of the stern cleats held a scuba tank against the port gunwale. I nested my tank behind the cord and took the rest of my gear into the cabin.

There was a head on the port side and a cramped galley on the starboard where I put my water bottles in the sink. Two settees faced a table that obviously could be combined into a double bunk by uprooting the table post. Off-shore rods were racked overhead. Hanging lockers marked the entrance to the forecastle, where I dumped my wet suit, mask and fins on the deck with a jumble of rubber boots, foul weather overalls and jackets. One of the vee berths was stacked with tackle boxes, rolls of leader wire, spools of monofilament and a coil of nylon line. In the other, a twisted sleeping bag confirmed that these were bachelor quarters. I listened a moment to make sure Dutch was still on the foredeck securing the dinghy, and then I pulled out the drawers under the settees: miscellaneous spare parts and tackle in one, dryer-wrinkled shorts, socks, khakis and tee shirts in the other. Port side hanging locker held a couple of shirts with collars, a blue blazer, gray slacks and black loafers. I tried the starboard hanging locker: locked.

When I heard Dutch edging past the cabin I opened one of the bottles of water and slid under the table onto the starboard settee. He hopped down into the cockpit and came through the companionway flashing that public relations smile. "Comfort time." He opened the little refrigerator, stowed my water and took out a beer. "Join me?"

I held up my bottle of water and shook my head. "Not till we bring up that cannon. What else do you think is down there?"

He slid into the settee opposite me. "Guy that hired me, he wore a gold coin." Holding up his hand, thumb and index finger making a circle, "Big one. He said he got it from the guy that found this wreck."

"Some guy found the wreck, but just left it there?"

He shrugged.

I waited. He fired up a Camel. Finally, I leaned over on one cheek, fished out my wallet and extracted the bills I'd drawn from the ATM. I counted five twenties into a stack and moved it aside, counted five more and then five more. When I looked up he broke his stare from the money and met my eyes. "Before we go out, I'd like to hear everything you know about this guy," I said. "Then, if it sounds like it's worth the trip, I'll pay in advance. The whole charter fee. How's that?"

He looked back at the three stacks of bills, rubbing one finger across the grain of his dark stubble, and then reignited the smile. "Partner, you sure know how to seal a deal." He tilted his head back and tipped the beer can toward the overhead.

Then, wiping one knuckle under his mouth and pulling down a chestful of smoke, he began: "His name is Doubles. Joey Doubles. When I came into Key West they were already here, Joey and that little prick tease he traveled with."

CHAPTER 9
Dutch's Story

"My charter business down there – the name of the place, you don't need that, okay?" Dutch arched those sun-blond eyebrows and shook his head, answering for me. "It was mostly shark fishing. Taking guys out, setting up a chum slick, hooking into a big meat eater – lotta guys, they have something to prove, y'know what I'm saying? But now the commercial boats are out catching sharks on long lines, just cutting the fins to sell the chinks for soup. How're you going to compete with ten miles of hooks behind one boat? Too many days coming back empty – my business was turning to shit."

He slid out of the settee and took the two steps into the galley. "Just to get by, I got myself involved in, let's call it a commodity transaction. Sure you don't want a beer?"

I shook my head and held up the remains of my bottle of water. "Deal turned sour," he went on, rattling around in the refrigerator. "All of a sudden it was time for me to move on. Sort of in a hurry."

He came back with a fresh Rolling Rock and scooted in across from me. "But with the fucking Arabs goosing up the price of diesel and one thing and another, by the time I got to Key West I was running on fumes and macaroni."

He popped open the can and took a short pull, looking out through the companionway behind me with a smile, as if recalling some youthful prank. "I'd been hanging around the docks for a few days, every now and then picking up a half-day charter that the regular boats didn't have room for. I was making just enough to get by but not enough to get out of there when this guy came along, and he didn't even want to go fishing. Wanted someone to take him diving. Just him, alone."

I asked, "What'd he look like?"

He snorted a little laugh. "Like he was all tricked out for some kind of a show. Big black moustache and a scarf around his neck – looked like silk, y'know what I'm saying? – with a big gold coin on a chain."

"Real gold?"

He shrugged. "Looked real to me. But like I say, I was in no mood to – if he was a charter, he was pure gold to me."

"Kind of odd though, wasn't it?" I probed. "You wonder why he didn't just go out on one of the dive boats?"

Dutch shook his head slowly with a patient expression and then, in a tone that said he was going to explain this one more time: "I was ready to provide any service he wanted, y'know what I'm saying? Except maybe lip service – I never get *that* broke."

I nodded encouragement, and he went on: "He didn't ask me why I didn't have a mooring at the charter-boat dock, and I didn't ask him any chickenshit questions that weren't any of my business. He paid in advance, just like you. Him I had to ask, but he paid. So when I picked him up in my dink that afternoon I didn't tell him I'd already made the acquaintance of his shipmate."

He paused, waiting for a reaction. It occurred to me that Dutch, after a life on the margins at best and on the run at other times, was savoring his moment in front of an audience, if only an audience of one.

"I have this theory," he went on, gesturing with an open hand. "There's some women, I can look at her and tell where she lives, y'know what I'm saying? Lot of women, they live right behind their boobs. Those are the mothers. If you're hurt or sick, you want one of the boob ladies. Some women live behind their eyes – they're the teachers, or maybe the librarians. I never got along so hot with them. But an island woman I knew, she lived in her hands. Cook, sew, rub your shoulders at night. Wonderful hands. Fine woman. But this one, the one with Joey Doubles, just watch her walk down the street and you knew where she lived. Right between her legs."

I smiled and nodded audience reaction, and he went on: "I didn't say anything about her at the time, and neither did Joey Doubles. Kinda funny, now that I think about it – Princess Pussy was on both sides of that deal but neither one of us was talking about her. All Joey told me up front was that they'd already been trying to dive that site, him and the Princess. Neither one of them knew what they were doing, and so they couldn't find it. What I learned later, Joey was afraid, if they did find it – well, he didn't trust Princess Pussy and so he'd been out there trying to dive it by himself. Which was stupid, but like I say, he didn't know what he was doing."

He pulled down some more Rolling Rock and fished the pack from his shirt pocket. "But that was later," he said, tapping out a Camel and starting it with a paper match. "And anyway, I wasn't going to ask questions. The Princess had already told me what he was looking for. I figured he was going to have to tell me something, sooner or later, and I was interested to hear what he'd say. On the way out that afternoon he told me he was an art dealer. Antiquities. Not antiques – I had him say it twice so I could get it right – antiquities. I asked what that means, and he said, oh, like artifacts of the Spanish Main." Another pause for effect, exhaling two streams of smoke.

I repeated, "Spanish Main?" for audience reaction.

Portentous nod. "That's what he said. Like he was talking about, shit, I don't know – something ordinary. Picking up shells and coral scraps. So I said, like what comes out of shipwrecks? And he said like, those are always interesting artifacts.

"I told him I'm just a charter boat captain and I don't know squat about pirate gold. He kind of laughed and said it was a pleasure doing business with an honest man. And then he started talking about three, four hundred years ago, guys hauling treasure on mules – it was mostly silver, he said, from the mines in Peru – out through the jungle and over the mountains from Panama. When they got over on this side they loaded all that silver, and maybe some gold and other stuff they'd sweated out of the Indians, onto gallons."

"Gallons?" I said, and then, "Oh, galleons."

"Galleons – right. Just making sure you're paying attention. You know, clumsy old square riggers that had to beat against the trade winds to take the loot to Spain. And Drake and Henry Morgan and all those other tough sonsabitches were waiting for them. Hanging around in fast little ships to windward here in the Caribbean. Pirates captured a bunch and took the loot off to Jamaica, which was an English island then, but some of the treasure ships got sunk in the shootouts. And of course a bunch just broke up in storms or ran aground because their charts were no good and they didn't have any GPS or even Loran back then. Thousands of ships went down, one way or the other, according to Joey Doubles. Spilling treasure all over hell and gone."

He looked at his watch. "We're going to get out there at slack tide, we can't sit around bullshitting too much longer."

"I don't mind diving in moving water," I said. "Tell me some more about this guy Joey Doubles. He really seemed to know something about the treasure fleets?"

Dutch finished his beer and studied the can as if to find some truth hidden in the logo. "Truth is, I didn't know what to make of Joey. He looked like one of those corny old movie stars, you know, the neck scarf and the clipped moustache and all. But when it came to that treasure stuff, I had to believe he was for real, y'know what I'm saying? He didn't have a lot of scuba experience, but he knew his way around a boat, all right. I believed him when he said he and Puss had been bopping around the islands. I didn't ask how he got hold of those numbers, because I already knew."

He hitched forward on the settee and put his elbows on the table. "Tell you the truth, where I'm taking you isn't absolutely virgin. And I don't want you to think we'll go out and just start picking up pieces of eight. Like I told you, all I saw was the fluke of an anchor and what looks like it might be an old cannon, all crusted up. Joey, he said he was interested in antiquities, but I don't think that meant old anchors and cannons. I think if we start sifting around in that sand – but I'm not promising anything, y'know what I'm saying?"

"What about the woman?" I prompted. "How does she figure in all this?"

Dutch leaned back with the smile of a raconteur. "Princess Puss? Thought you'd be curious about her. Well, it was when I'd only been in Key West two or three days. That morning I'd been hanging around the dock looking for a charter but there was nothing doing, and so around nine I rowed back out to the *Treat*. Thought I'd build a pot of coffee and rig some ballyhoo and then go back in around eleven to see if I could pick up something for the afternoon. But when I got around the stern to where my ladder was, there, all snubbed up so it wouldn't show from the beach, was this dinghy."

"She went aboard your boat?"

He ignored that as just an interruption in the story flow. "Well shit, everything I had was aboard the boat. But on the other hand, none of it was worth stealing. I decided none of it was worth a scuffle with whoever was scrounging through it, and so I really didn't want to surprise somebody into something unnecessary. I thought about just rowing back into the dock and having steak and eggs at the Cuban, but then I realized I couldn't even afford the Cuban, which made me kind of cranky and so I called out, 'Hello, the boat'.

"'Hello, the cutest little dinghy in Key West,' she says walking out into the cockpit, and, well, that turned into one hell of an interesting morning. Not just finding where she lives – that didn't take long – and going there, although that involved detours and side trips and, well, never mind about that. When the boat had stopped rocking and I'd settled down onto an even keel again too, she started talking about how she brought that treasure site to Joey Doubles."

"She knew where it was?" I said, remembering what she'd told me in Harry's bedroom.

He dropped the cigarette butt into the empty can. "According to her, she got it from a sweet old man who loved her. Took up with him down in Curacao. I asked her about the place, you know, to kinda check what she was telling me, and sure enough, she described those silly outboard motors that swing the bridge back and forth across the harbor. She said this old guy was into the stories of the Spanish Main. Read all kinds of weird books and records – he'd study until three in the morning and then be back at it when she brought him his lime juice and aspirin."

"How'd he get it?"

Dutch shook his head. "She said she didn't know just when the old man found this treasure site, but he must not have been in the best of health at the time because he decided not to try to recover it then. I guess a man with the patience to study all those old records is not going to rush things when he's found what he's been looking for. Instead, he went to Curacao to get over whatever he thought was wrong with him.

"When Gisu knew him, he'd come to realize that what he'd caught was old age. Couldn't get it up except when she gave him her special attention. Which I understood – that woman could turn wet line into bar stock. The old guy was so grateful that, before he slipped away into what she called a kind of twilight, he gave her the numbers.

"Now–" he made a fist for emphasis "–what she needed was a boat and somebody to help her bring up whatever is down there. Joey Doubles had something going in the Antilles. Gisu didn't know what it was – you know, Curacao isn't Port au Prince. If there *is* any action around there, it's in Aruba. But whatever Joey had going down in Curacao, he came ashore off that nice little seaworthy boat with that pretty moustache and that sexy scarf and those RayBan shades and well, as Gisu said, that's her kinda guy. She just couldn't resist alpha males, she said, and here she comes onto me again. So, by the time the morning was over it was kinda understood that we were a team."

"What about Joey Doubles?"

Dutch raised one finger, lecturing. "You see, she never really did trust Joey, and it turned out she was right. Soon as he thought she'd put him on the site he started looking for a way to leave her behind. Said he needed a man with some experience, somebody could help him get the anchor in just the right place to hold the boat over the numbers and then get in the water with him – Gisu was afraid to go down with a tank.

"But the charter boats figure their day rates on six fishermen, which made the price too steep for Joey. He'd tried to negotiate – explained that they weren't going to burn fuel swinging on the pick out there – but they're getting full charters most every day and so they weren't interested. So then he started leaving her ashore and diving by himself. She figures, when he finds what he's looking for, he's outta here.

"But like I say, Gisu didn't trust Joey from the beginning, and so the numbers she gave him, she'd changed them a little. Not enough to be obvious, but enough so he'd need her to find the spot. Of course, she could put team Dutch-Gisu right on top of it. That's what she said. Except that Joey was a problem. If he kept diving out there, he was close enough that he might just happen on the goodies by himself. And of course if Gisu and I showed up in the neighborhood – well, Joey might look like a sweetheart but he never liked to share, and he had a black temper.

"Which is where *I* come in. Joey doesn't really like diving by himself – he's not *that* stupid – and now here I am in Key West, just picking up charter scraps. Old Dutch ought to be willing to take him out for a reasonable price."

He nodded a knowing wink. "I was beginning to see where Gisu was going with this, but I wanted to hear her spell it out. I didn't have to go there, where she wanted to take me, y'know what I'm saying? But she had me curious. And she had a way of making the god*damnedest* things sound ordinary as 'pass the salt.' I mean, that story about the old guy in Curacao and the treasure numbers – when I try to tell you about him it sounds off the bulkhead, but when Gisu told it, well, I could understand how Joey would be out there diving.

"Anyway, when she explained how we were going to deal with the problem of Joey it was just casual, like she was telling me how to get to the Laundromat. She says I take him where he wants to go and let him go down to muck around. Then I just pick up the anchor and head for Big Pine. Nobody's going to miss a transient boat that was paying day-rates for the mooring.

She'll rent a car and be up here the next day. With *Happy Daze* still in the harbor, nobody's going to go looking for either one of them for days. Probably not for weeks, and by that time we'll have the goodies and be living high off the hog somewhere.

"She was sitting just where you are now. Course, we had the table up and all this was a bed, but she was sitting there in the corner with the sun making her glow, kind of, with those incredible boobs of hers, both looking outboard, and that Sunday-school smile. But those tilted black eyes, they could see right through to what I was thinking. She says we can trust each other because neither one of us can do this without the other, so that makes us a team."

"And Joey," I said, "he's just going to be treading water out there somewhere."

The lecturing finger came up again. "On the way to Key West, Joey was a teammate. Now he's just a solved problem. And me, I'm going to be the teammate on the way to Big Pine, and then what? I figured I had a pretty good idea.

"But I played along. Asked what time of day he liked to go out and she said it depended on the tide, he liked to be in the water at slack. I said I'd like to go out before first light, when nobody's around who could say, 'Last time I saw Joey he was going out on that *Dutch Treat*.' She said that would be a problem, because Joey liked to smoke a little weed or snort a little dust of an evening and then sleep in, most days. Maybe if I took him out a time or two I could persuade him that early morning was diver's light, or some such bullshit, because what Joey knew about diving he learned right here in Key West with the tourists.

"I said I don't know, it all sounds interesting but Key West is too rich for my blood and I don't know how I can afford to hang around here waiting for Joey to decide he wants me to take him out. She gave me a look out of the corners of those see-through eyes that said she'd been wondering when this was coming. She kind of hitched forward like she was telling me a secret and said she'd found a nice little high-stakes game run by a dealer off the casino boat who'd become a dear friend. So – and I remember she moved her shoulders to shimmy those boobs when she said this – she had a little investment capital. Just a little.

"We talked about how much I needed to cover expenses. Dickered a little, and finally settled on a thousand up front and then ten thousand in Big Pine, when Joey was flotsam on the Gulf Stream. After that, it would be fifty-fifty on what we could bring up from the wreck. She said partnerships are based on trust but it's just good manners to cut the deck, and so when we met in Big Pine I should bring that gold coin Joey wore. I said I didn't want to be trying to take something off him, but she said not to worry, in that dive class they told him that barracuda are attracted to jewelry and so he always left the coin on the boat. Only time he ever took it off was when he dived."

Dutch raised both palms. "What was I going to say, that I didn't have any use for ten big ones? I don't know what I expected, but it didn't cost anything to play along. She told me to wait for her at the casino boat landing that night, and – what d'you know? – there she was, mixed in with about a dozen others waiting to get rid of some of their money. She slipped me an envelope and told me to be on the pier tomorrow morning after Joey gets his coffee and aspirin down and I'd get a charter. She goes on, with that sweet little smile as if we were just making conversation, that tomorrow afternoon she'd be in her private game but her cell phone number's in the envelope. She said I could call her on my way back to Big Pine Key and we'd meet in the parking lot – bound to be a parking lot somewhere around the docks.

"I said not so fast, I wanted to set up a trip at first light, remember? She said she thought maybe I might decide to move a little faster, and when was I going to look in the envelope? I opened it enough to fan those ten Ben Franklins, and whatever she saw on my face made her laugh. She said there's a hundred more of those when I got to Big Pine Key, and that's just the start.

"About then the purser came down to the foot of the gangway and Gisu started moving with the others to go aboard. She said if you *do* decide to care of business tomorrow, don't forget to bring the doubloon along to Big Pine so she'll know Joey's enjoying a swim."

Dutch smiled at my reaction and held up one hand. "Course, I never intended to leave that guy out there in the drink. But now that I'd seen the color of her money, the idea of another ten thousand just for showing up at Big Pine Key, well that was something I had to think about. On one hand, I was already way ahead of the game, y'know what I'm saying? I had a thousand in my pocket after an afternoon in the sack that I was going to remember when I was as old as her guy in Curacao. All I had to do was just shove off for parts north, wham, bam, thank you ma'am.

"But it seemed a shame to walk away from ten big ones. By the time I got back aboard the *Treat* I still hadn't made up my mind. I finally decided it didn't cost anything to see if Joey showed up looking for a charter the next morning. If he didn't show, then by the time Gisu was out of her private game I could be underway and she'd be just a sweet memory."

"But he showed up," I put in.

Dutch nodded. "Fussy black moustache, silk scarf and all. He asked if that was my sport fish on the mooring and when I said it was he wanted to book me for what was left of the day. He took that treasure diving seriously, y'know what I'm saying? He had a chart that he'd lined off in grids, and he gave me the GPS numbers that would put my anchor right in the middle of one. On the way out, that was when he told me about the treasure ships and all that, and by the time I had the anchor down I was thinking about those gold crosses studded with emeralds that I'd seen in Mel Fisher's museum, and those gold chains and all the silver coins and stuff. If I hadn't known that Gisu had put us in the wrong place I'd have been ready to get right in there and start looking, y'know what I'm saying?

"As it was, I helped him get into his gear – he hung that doubloon chain over a rod holder – and watched him go over the side and start down the anchor line. We were in about fifty feet, but the visibility was good because that squall hadn't blown through yet. I sat up on the fly bridge, drank a beer, watched a frigate bird bully a tern or whatever into dropping his fish while I tried to figure out why I was feeling bad about having him down there by himself. Wasn't my fault that Gisu was conning him. And my charter was just to take him out here, that's all. Nothing said about getting wet.

"But fifty feet is a lot of water when it's on top of you, and it's not a good idea to be under it by yourself. I kept leaning over the bridge, trying to see down the anchor line, and thinking about what Gisu had said. She'd just changed the numbers a little, so it wouldn't be obvious, and if he kept diving out here he might find what he was looking for.

"I kept thinking, what if I got in the water with him? She said he didn't share and he had a black temper, but he didn't seem like that kind of a guy. He'd been so glad to find a skipper who'd take him out that he'd told me all about the treasure fleet, and wasn't that sharing? If I got down there with him and then we found the treasure, why, I had to believe Joey would at least be good for a nice tip. When I saw the anchor line move I climbed down and went forward to where I could look straight into the blue Gulf Stream, and there he was, hanging on about halfway up the line while he depressurized. I can't explain this, but I was glad to see he was okay, and by the time he'd come up I had my own tank and gear in the cockpit. Maybe I was hoping Joey and I would find the treasure so I wouldn't have to figure out what to do about Gisu. Who knows what makes a man do the dumb things he does, y'know what I'm saying?

"I thought Joey might tell me to stay in the boat, just to make sure I didn't have any claim on what we found, but no – he slapped my shoulder and said how glad he was to have me with him down there because this was deeper than he'd ever worked before, and he really needed a dive partner. When he'd finished his sector this time and was heading back to the anchor line, he said a whole section of sea floor just lifted up and drifted off into the murk. Joey almost bolted to the surface, even though he knew better, but then it tilted a little so he could see the white belly and he realized it was just a big ray that had been buried up to its eyes, waiting for dinner.

"I told him this was deep for me too – I just keep a tank on the boat for picking up lobsters, and twelve or fourteen feet is plenty for that – but I'd take it slow on the way down and see how my gear took the depth. What I meant was, see I how felt with all that water on top of me.

"Well, turns out, what I felt was – scared. When the color started changing I started listening to my breath. Seemed like the sound changed as I sank out of the warm surface water. Every breath seemed to be giving me less air. I got down to maybe fifteen feet above Joey, who was finning along the bottom. I tried to stay calm, but I couldn't help trying to remember the last time I'd had the valves and regulator checked. Then I noticed that my mask was leaking.

"I looked up. The surface was, you know, like a crackly mirror and it looked close. Now I was gasping at what was trickling through my hose. Ever had your air cut off? Not a good time for calm analysis. Before I realized it, I was kicking up toward the light, balls out. Joey must have shoved off the bottom like a rocket to get up to me fast as he did. When he grabbed my ankle I tried to kick him off, but he went up my leg hand over hand and got his arm around my neck. I was thrashing so wild I didn't see what he had in his hand until he shoved it right in my face. It was his mouthpiece.

"I spit out mine and grabbed his, sucking in that sweet air. After I'd settled down he pointed toward the anchor line. I took a big breath, gave him his air back and we both swam over to the line. Then he gave it back to me and swam around to where he could look at my tank and regulator. I could feel him working at something, and then he came around, tried my mouthpiece and turned thumbs up. We swapped again and then, sweet Jesus, I was getting air out of my own tank again.

"He pointed to his watch and I nodded that I understood. While we waited out the decompression I wondered what he'd done to fix my air. Couldn't have been much, because he was just back there the time of one held breath. Maybe he just shook the tank to make me feel like he was doing something, because what was wrong with my air supply was just panic. What ever, it worked.

"When we came back up we didn't talk much. Joey marked off one of the grids on his chart and asked if I'd take him out tomorrow. Shit, what was I going to say? The man had shared his *air* with me. We agreed to go out at ten in the morning.

"When we came back into the harbor and Joey was waiting

on the foredeck to pick up the mooring, I could see Gisu in the cockpit of *Happy Daze*. Joey retrieved the doubloon and then we loaded both tanks into his inflatable for recharging. He said something about treasure day tomorrow and gave me a little salute as he shoved off and started rowing away. In *Happy Daze*, Gisu gave me something that I don't think was a salute."

He looked at his watch again. "You want to hear the rest of this, I could tell you on the way out."

I hesitated a moment but decided that Dutch was enjoying the telling so much that I was going to get the whole story either way, and so I shoved the three stacks of twenties across the table and said, "Let's go for a swim."

Dutch stood, stuffing the bills into his pocket. "We haul ass, we can have two, maybe three hours in the water before dark. You want to cast us off?"

When we were underway I climbed up to the bridge. He showed me the chart with the search grids. As I studied it I noticed the shoals where we'd hidden *Bottom Line* behind the mangroves. I imagined Marge tilting her head back to laugh at the idea that she'd been mistaken for Gisu. When we left the harbor and he throttled up to cruising speed I sat on the padded bench along the port side. Dutch punched a way point and a destination into the GPS and sat in the chair. I didn't have to ask him to go on with the story.

"Like I was saying," he said, checking the summer cumulus on the horizon to the west, "the next day when the anchor was down in the next grid and we got ready to dive, I made an excuse. Said that first I wanted to look at my prop where I'd dinged it on a coral head last week. He said sure, but how about we could hook up a safety line so he could give a jerk if he needed help. After that, I didn't go below the place where the temperature and colors change, but we stayed connected to the line. He never gave a jerk, but I just hung around near the surface where I could keep an eye on him and count how many kinds of fish I could name while he did the treasure hunting, and we – neither one of us said anything about my panic attack.

"He wasn't going to embarrass me, y'know what I'm saying? I knew I was going to have to tell him something about Gisu, what she was up to. I owed him that – shit, Joey had shared his air with me, and now suppose Gisu found some other guy who needed a quick buck, y'know what I'm saying? But there was something about Joey, going out there every day searching that ocean floor grid by grid, I mean, this was a guy who had a *purpose*. You just knew that anything getting in his way, well, I remembered what Gisu said, that he had a black temper. I figured telling him about her was going to make trouble."

He shook his head slowly, remembering. "And it did. It sure as shit did.

"It was the day of that squall that I told him. There was another boat messing around out there that day, and Joey thought it must be Gisu. Thought she'd hired somebody to come check us out, which made no sense because it was Gisu's numbers we were diving around in the first place so she didn't have to come looking for us. But Joey went kind of apeshit, and we chased that boat clear off into the flats.

"While I was bucking us through those water mountains – I mean, it got *rough*, and in a *hurry* – I was thinking that if I didn't tell him about what Gisu was up to pretty soon, when I finally *did* tell him he'd be pissed at me for waiting so long, and so when that other boat – she didn't draw as much water as we did, and whoever it was took her back onto the flats behind some islands where we couldn't follow. Joey wanted to wait a while for her to come back out into the channel, and that's when I told him."

He paused, and I said, "How'd he take it?"

"Joey just listened. Didn't ask any questions. When I told him about Gisu showing up on my boat he smiled a little and nodded, like this had happened before, but when I got to the old guy in Curacao he shook his head, like he couldn't believe what he was hearing. And then when I told him she'd changed the GPS numbers a little he twisted his mouth and nodded, like he was saying he should have known. At the end, where she says I should leave Joey out there and meet her in Big Pine Key, he just looked at me like, no shit? Still listening. I told him that Gisu had been watching us tie up in the harbor every evening and looking kind of impatient. I figured I didn't have to say that maybe she'd be looking for another teammate before long.

"Joey looked over at the islands where that boat was still hiding, and then he said, 'You know what Gisu needs? Gisu needs to see a ghost.' I could tell that Joey was so pissed he wanted to do something crazy, like jump out of the boat with a knife in his teeth and go after Gisu – he still thought she had to have something to do with that boat over there behind the islands – but he never lost his cool. Like when I was fighting my air hose but he – well, Joey just never lost it, no matter what happened. He had a *purpose*.

"So, just cool as collins he asked me if I believed her, about sharing the treasure, and I said of course not, but I hated to leave those ten big ones on the table. He nodded and said I'd earned a bonus sure enough, and if we both went to go pick it up, then while we were about it we could probably get the treasure numbers too. The real ones.

"We decided the squall had stirred up the bottom so bad there was no point trying to dive, and even Gisu would know that. Joey kept staring at the islands. He said a day off would give him a chance to find out whose boat that was, just in case Gisu's making promises to other guys. When we got in he'd tell Gisu that somebody tried to follow us and so we're taking a day off, but the next day we'll be out before first light, when we can be sure we'll have the dive site to ourselves.

"He asked me again if that was the signal – before first light – and I said when she heard that she'd figure the game was on, but I didn't trust her to keep her end of the bargain. Joey said don't worry, she'll show up. She'll want to see that doubloon, make sure Joey's no problem any more. When she hands over the ten thousand, he said, I just tap the horn and this is gonna be fun, watching her face. He said he'd wrap a little sea weed around his neck and come to the car rolling his eyes. He started practicing drowned man expressions, and we both broke up. That Joey, he's a cool one."

Dutch stood and peered at the track line on the scope, and then he shoved a little more way on the boat. The sea was almost flat and over my left shoulder I could see the bow wave peeling off into foam. I knew I wanted to have a look behind that locked door in the cabin before we got to the dive site, but I didn't want to interrupt the story at this point.

When Dutch sat down again he went on: "After we've had our parking lot reunion, Joey says we'll all three go out and find that treasure. He said he was always planning to split it down the middle, and he'd a lot rather split it with me than with her. Then he kind of laughed and said, of course he didn't want to be ungrateful. If Gisu is really helpful, takes us right to the spot without any bitching and moaning, then he'd give her air fare back to Curacao. Out of his own share. 'I can't help it,' he said, 'but I'm just sentimental.' He mugs another face, and when we pull up the anchor and head back into Key West we're laughing and trying to guess what she'll do when she sees Joey's ghost with the seaweed in its hair.

"The next day I paid off my mooring, topped off my tanks and laid in some groceries. At high noon, when I figured a dozen people already knew I was leaving town, I cast off and made a point to wave goodbye to the guys around the charter boat dock. I took my time getting out of the harbor and running up the coast to Stock Island. I stopped for lunch at that Mex place that caters to tourists and told the waitress who brought my Dos Equis that I was headed up island. When I shoved off again I figured I'd left a trail a mile wide. Of course, that wouldn't matter if everything went the way Joey said it would, but I figured I might as well play it safe. Once we had that treasure in the boat, I wasn't sure Joey would just give Gisu traveling money, like he said, and kiss her goodby. I figured whatever he did would be his business, but by that time I wanted to be long gone, as far as anybody else knew."

Dutch lit another cigarette and I asked, "How much farther to where we're going?"

He glanced at the scope. "We've got a ways to go yet. You getting tired of sea stories?"

"No, but I think I'll go to the head."

He thumbed a gesture. "It's aft, behind the galley."

In the cabin I used the head and then tried the locked door again. I looked around the galley until I found an old paring knife that had been whet-stoned down to a skinny blade the size of a willow leaf that I could fit into the key hole. After a little probing I felt the lock turn. Inside the hanging locker was a miscellany of wash pants, a couple of collared shirts, a tropical weight blue blazer with the worn cuffs showing white lining, and a pair of topsiders. I was thinking about what Dutch had said about having nothing worth stealing as I fumbled behind the clothes and touched something cool and slick, which turned out to be a double-barrel 12 gauge shotgun that had been leaning against the bulkhead in the back.

Not surprising, I decided. Dutch had said his charter business had been shark fishing, which required a gin pole to get a couple of hundred pounds out of the water and then a gun to quiet it down, because no sensible captain puts a live shark in the boat. But I didn't like the idea of being alone with him and a loaded gun, and so I broke the shotgun open and took the two shells out of the breech. Groping around behind the shoes I found a box of shells, almost full. I checked the load: fours. Heavy enough to drill, at point-blank range, holes the size of half dollars through the cartilaginous skull of a shark. Or anything organic.

I put the gun back and closed the locker, but the knife wouldn't turn the lock the other way. I put the two shells back in the box and went into the forecastle. From the tangle of gear on the port vee berth I extracted a sea boot, stuffed the box of shells into the toe and buried it back in the disorder.

While I was there I looked around for something out of place. Unmade sleeping bag in one berth, foul-weather gear and tackle on the other, my fins, wet suit and mask on the deck. I looked into the chain locker and then, under a fraying wetsuit piled against the after bulkhead, I found a mesh bag. Inside were fins, a mask and a leaded belt. A vague sense of something wrong nagged at me, but I filed it away and went back into the cabin to focus on what I would do when we got to the dive site.

Standing in the companionway and watching the wake spread across the suddenly ink-blue water, I decided: first, make sure that Dutch is always in the water with me. What would I do if I looked around and he's not there? He could be back on board in seconds. If he brought the ladder up after him, he could take all time he needed to cut off the anchor and leave me behind. I couldn't think of any plausible reason why he'd do that, but I still didn't like the possibility that he could.

I considered trying to find a way to take the ignition key with me over the side. As we approached the site, I'd expect Dutch to put me on the foredeck, waiting to let go the anchor on his signal. When he shut off the engine and came down to get ready to dive, what excuse could I create to go back up to the flying bridge? Trying to think of something, it occurred to me that Dutch surely had an emergency set of keys hidden somewhere on the boat, anyway.

If I was afraid to leave the key in the boat, then what was I doing out here in the first place? Target fixation, Harry would say. But I could see that brass cannon in my mind's eye, and where there was a brass cannon there would surely be other things that have been waiting out here three hundred years. Waiting for me.

I climbed back up to the flying bridge. The track on the GPS scope was approaching the destination mark, and I wondered how much longer this story was going to take. "So," I said, "you went to Stock Island."

He shook his head. "Went right on past, up to Sugarloaf Key. Poked around the north side there until I found a little cove where I could get my anchor down just outside somebody's mullet net. I watched the sun make that dive into the sea while I charcoaled a steak on the fantail grill, and I hit the sack early so I'd be ready to get underway in time to get back down there before first light. I kept thinking about what Mel Fisher says – you know, in the brochure they give you? – what he says about seeing the ocean bottom paved with gold coins. I guess I still thought Joey's treasure was just kind of scattered around there on top of the sand. But, hell, how was I to know what the wreck site is really like?

"Anyway, the next morning I felt my way from buoy to buoy down to Key West and eased up alongside *Happy Daze* in that pearly light before dawn. Joey was in the cockpit, but there was no sign of Gisu. He didn't say a word, just loaded our tanks and climbed aboard. When he shoved us off I checked the harbor to see if anybody was moving around in any of the other boats, and that's when I noticed a burned-out hulk still smoking on a mooring close to the docks.

"As we left the harbor Joey climbed up to the flying bridge and said he didn't get much sleep last night. Boat caught on fire in the harbor, he said, and people were running around like Mardi Gras. I told him I'd found a quiet cove on the way to Big Pine where he could get a nap – no reason to really go off shore – and I asked what Gisu was up to. He said she was acting like this was just another day but he knew she wouldn't be far from her cell phone, and was there a phone in that cove? I said there's nothing there but a soggy old net, but I could raise the marine operator on the radio and she'd patch a call through for us. He asked could we stop for breakfast along the way. I couldn't say that I didn't want to be seen with him, and so instead I said that when I'd stocked up yesterday I'd bought half a dozen eggs and if he wanted to hold the helm I'd go down and scramble them up. By the time I dropped anchor in the Sugarloaf cove again, cool Joey was fed and sound asleep in a vee berth.

"I fiddled around, casting a bucktail into the tide in case somebody came along and wondered why a boat was in there, and trying to keep from thinking about what I would do with a bunch of sudden money. After an hour or so, when we still had the cove to ourselves and the cormorants, I opened up the engine hatch and crawled around down there a while, checking dip sticks and hose clamps and seal packing. Still he slept."

Dutch gestured around the bridge. "I climbed up here and got out my charts. If something went wrong, there's islands north of Big Pine that look like nothing but flats and bars and reefs. Cudjoe Key, Torch Key and Johnson Key – they all looked like places where a careful man could tuck a boat out of sight and slap mosquitos while he waited for things to settle down before he started on to Naples or Ft. Myers. At ten o'clock I went down and woke Joey.

"He got up relaxed and rested, which made me feel more fagged out and wound too tight. While I waited for him to go to the head and climb up on the bridge with me, I fished Gisu's cell phone number out of my wallet and then I lit up the radio. It took a while to get through, but when we finally heard her phone she answered the first ring, coming through the speaker hollow but loud.

"I tried to explain that I was on my ship-to-shore, which means I'm broadcasting over the air and so you should be a little careful what you say, but our date is on. She said that's good, and how's our friend? I don't want to talk about that on the air and so I say that her signal's breaking up but I'll meet her for lunch. She says maybe she can't make that – she has to go ashore, get a cab over to Simonton and rent a car and then drive up to Big Pine. So we settle on twelve thirty."

Dutch stood up and, with his eyes on the GPS display, pulled the throttles back to half speed. "Coming up on the mark. You want to go down and drop the anchor when we're on it – I'll tell you the rest of the story while we're getting into our gear."

I climbed down and sidestepped past the cabin onto the foredeck. There was only enough wind to stir the surface, and when Dutch gave the signal the anchor spiraled straight down through the slack tide, out of sight into the blue. Plenty of water to keep a shallow-draft ship afloat. But maybe the Spaniard had hit a coral head and turned back, trying to make land in the Keys before she sank. Or maybe a desperate sea chase ended here with the Spaniard holed and sinking, or perhaps scuttled, before the privateers could board.

Dutch backed down on the anchor to make sure it was holding before he turned off the engines and climbed down to the cabin. "Bottom looks a little different on the depth finder," he said. "Maybe I was just swinging different on the anchor but I wonder – maybe my GPS is drifting a little."

"What looks different?" I asked, starting to peel down. I was watching to make sure he didn't open the jimmied hanging locker.

"More contour," he said, going past me to rummage through the disorder in the forecastle. "Unless maybe that's wreck structure showing on the scope. It was still a little gloomy down there when I found it. Could be I didn't see it all."

"So tell me," I said, "what happened after you talked to Gisu?"

He came out with a frayed wet suit that he tossed on the settee as he started undressing. "I wanted to start slapping high fives, but Joey was still dead serious. I mean, that guy never took his eye off the ball. He said Gisu would remember about going out before first light, what that meant, and so what if she already had the car rented and ready to go? What if that stuff about not being able to get up here by noon was just so she could get to Big Pine first and watch me come ashore, make sure I was alone? We talked about that and looked at the chart – there didn't seem to be any place I could put Joey ashore except right there in the harbor – and so I firewalled the boat, got alongside the dock a little after eleven and dropped Joey off. He said he'd find some place out of sight around the parking lot and wait. He told me not to look around, but he'd be watching."

Dutch paused while we both put our arms and heads through our wet suit tops and pulled them down. When we emerged he went on: "I went back out to the boat, got underway and hove to a couple of miles off shore. I policed up the boat a little to keep my mind off what might happen when Joey had what he wanted from Gisu and we were off shore. While I was hosing down the cockpit I noticed the two scuba tanks. I stowed Joey's out of sight forward, just in case Gisu was watching with binoculars as I came in. At noon I was back in the harbor and rowing the dinghy in to the dock, thinking I could feel her eyes on the back of my neck."

Hopping around on one foot and then the other, we wriggled into the clinging rubber pants. Dutch sat on the settee and I opened another bottle of water. "So there she was," I guessed. "Waiting for you."

He shook his head. "There was only half a dozen cars in the parking lot. Couple empty boat trailers, and four or five gulls cracking mussels. I sat on one of the trailers and watched the gulls. Each one had his own drop zone. He'd rise up eight or ten feet, just high enough so that he could get back down before the other gull could get over and poach, and drop his mussel. Then he'd sink down, pick it up and drop it again. If he'd dropped from fifteen or twenty feet, the mussel would probably have popped right open, but he couldn't risk losing it to the other gull. I named one of them Joey and the other Gisu and made a bet with myself that Joey would score first."

Dutch looked at his watch in a bit of stage business. "I checked my watch and it was 12:42. Gisu broke open the mussel and flew away with the prize at 12:51, which left Joey rising and dropping and royally pissed off, and I began to chew the inside of my cheek. The next time I checked the time it was almost 1:00, and then I heard a whistle."

He drew a line in the air over the table. "Understand – A1A is the only road into and out of Big Pine, and there wasn't a car in sight. In the far corner of that empty parking lot there's an old fashioned telephone booth, y'know the clear plastic kind with a folding door? And there's Joey." Dutch waved a beckoning gesture.

"So I crunched through the goddam gulls' drop zone over to where he's standing and he says something's wrong. Like, I want to say, 'No shit?' but he goes on about Gisu, says she wouldn't be late for a date with the treasure so I should call her again.

"This time the phone rang three times before she answered. I asked where she was and she said on her way and I asked what's the problem and she asked if we were on the radio and I told her I was calling from a phone booth and she asked, where's Joey? I said the last time I saw him he was treading water, and so what's the problem with you?

"Joey stuck his head inside the booth so he could hear, and she said that if Joey's in the water, then she doesn't have a problem. I didn't look at Joey, just said something like, so, you ready to pick up some pieces of eight? And she says, been there, done that."

Sitting on the edge of the settee in his wet suit, Dutch tossed a gesture. "So I say something clever, like 'Huh?' and she laughs and says we're just one day late – they went out yesterday and picked it up. Which I don't believe because I was out in that storm, and so I say something about how murky it was the day after, and she says something about knowing right where to look.

"And then–" Dutch shot me a look that asked, are you ready for this? "–she said, 'What there *was* to find, which was hardly worth the trip.' Turns out, she's telling me now, the old guy in

Curacao had been feeding her a little line. So he could keep feeding her a little hose. But she said it was swell of me to take Joey for a swim, and she'd remember me in her will." He stood up and went into the forecastle.

I called after him, "You mean, that's it? She left you holding the bag?"

In a moment he came out, lugging his tank and gear. "She said you gotta know when to fold 'em, and the game was always too fast for me anyway."

I squeezed past him into the forecastle and collected my own gear. "You must have been royally pissed," I said when I came out.

Dutch snorted another of his little nose laughs. "Actually, I think I was a little relieved. I didn't know what was going to happen – I didn't really want to be around when Joey caught up with Gisu."

I followed Dutch out into the cockpit and spread out my gear alongside his. "How did Joey take it?" I asked.

"For just a minute there he almost lost his cool. He banged his fist in his palm and started talking about one fucking day late. He figured that boat we'd seen had to be Gisu – you know the boat I told you we chased? He figured she must have gotten on the site the next day. Even with everything roiled up, she got on it because she knew just where it was. Joey said he took care of the boat last night but he was just one fucking day late."

I strapped my knife on my left calf and my dive computer on my left wrist and shrugged into my inflatable vest as Dutch went on: "So off he went. I mean, that Joey is a man with *purpose*. We hustled into town, found a rental car place and the last I saw of him he was smoking up A1A to the Miami airport. Trying to get there before the next flight out to Curacao."

"Leaving you without the ten thousand," I said.

Rigged up now, except for mask and fins, Dutch sat on the gunwale and raised both palms. "I don't know if I ever did believe in that ten thousand. Joey gave me a hundred bucks and said, 'Remember what she said about her will? Well, she's going to need one sooner than she thinks.' So I figure I'm probably lucky to be out of it.

"When I went back to the boat I was hoping Gisu could get on a plane to Vegas or some place where Joey wouldn't find her, and also I was thinking about what she'd said about knowing where to look for the treasure. If she had the GPS numbers her friend – that's got to be the casino boat dealer, or maybe one of the rich conchs in the pot limit game he runs – whoever he is, he could probably drop anchor right on top of the wreck, I knew that. But the day after that squall, shit, ten or fifteen feet off the bottom the water had to be a sand slurry. Mel Fisher's best diver could sit on the deck of whatever's down there and he still couldn't see anything in that shit."

"You mean," I asked, trying to follow what he was saying, "you think she was leaving without…"

He nodded. "Without what they'd come for. After all that. Didn't seem likely, at first. But after I thought about it a while, I began to think, maybe so. With the dealer or whoever her friend was, now there was at least two of us looking to split the pot with her. And they'd already lost one boat in the deal, so maybe they were looking for something extra. Gisu was still the only one with the numbers. Maybe she figured she could come back some time after I was long gone. It's not like Key West is home, y'know what I'm saying? She figured I was just passing through, wouldn't be around long. Let old stupid Dutch do the disposal work, and you and me, dealer friend, we'll pick up the pieces. Pieces of eight.

"More I thought about it, the more I felt like Gisu had just been leading me around by my pecker. Then I remembered that Joey's search chart was still on the bridge, with only three grids left unmarked. Big Pine was a little farther north, but I could still get out there. Now that the water was clearing up, why not take a peek at those three grids?"

"By yourself?"

He shrugged. "Why not? I decided to try the middle one first – Joey would have taken them in order, a day at a time, but I don't do things by the book. I hadn't made up my mind to really search. Thought maybe I'd just poke around a little and then move on, but dumb luck beats smart, y'know what I'm saying? The first time I went down, there was the anchor fluke and that little snout of a cannon poking up out of the sand. Like I told you, I floundered around out there for a while trying to get a line to hold onto that cannon but every time I got back in the boat to take a strain on the gin pole the sling slipped off.

"So that's the story. You ready to go down and raise that cannon – maybe see what else we can find?"

CHAPTER 10
Looking at a Sharp Edge

As we worked our feet into the fins Dutch said, "Thing to look for is a white ball fender. I tied it onto the cannon with about fifteen feet of line, like a marker buoy, y'know what I'm saying? Find that, and we know we're on the wreck."

With our masks on the tops of our heads, I loaded his air bottle into his back harness and turned around to let him load mine. We strapped on lead belts, and I dropped mine to the deck once to test the release.

We pivoted on our butts to swing flippered feet over the water. "Sometimes I get a little spooked down there," he said. "Not like I did with Joey – not any more. I don't let it go that far. So just let me work in my own time, y'know what I'm saying?"

"We'll both work in our own time," I said. "Let's make the first dive a short one. Just look around and get the feel of the bottom."

We checked our regulators, seated the masks and flopped overboard together. I let myself sink fifteen or twenty feet, testing the regulator and tuning myself to the temperature and colors and the feeling of moving in three dimensions, and then I followed Dutch's flippers to the anchor line. We hung there a moment, exchanged a thumbs up and started down the line through a shoal of flashing silversides swarming around the nylon as if it were edible. We passed through a thermocline, all the colors but shades of blue beginning to bleach out, and I saw, or imagined, something glide away below us.

I felt a tap on my calf and looked around. Dutch was hanging onto the anchor line. I grabbed it below him and made a thumbs-up to ask, "you okay?" He signaled thumbs up and motioned for me to keep going down.

I hesitated, but instead of motioning "you first" I followed the line down to the Danforth anchor, flukes flat on top of a sponge-crusted boulder in the slack tide, and then finned along the broken floor. Glancing back, I saw Dutch following eight or ten feet above and behind me. I waved a signal for him to search the other side of the anchor, where I could see him, and he veered off around a rack of staghorn coral.

I had imagined coins glinting in the sand, but instead I was drifting over a tumble of boulders, fuzzed with some sort of feathery growth, and fan coral. An anemone waved its spines along the frontal lobe of a brain coral big enough for a whale's head. I looked around for Dutch. Sunlight, scattered by surface action, shafted through the blue murk. A doctor fish drifted past, staring from spectacled eyes. Beyond him a school of iridescent blue tangs performed close order drill. A tiny, chocolate damsel chased a blue and yellow wrasse three times its size away from damsel territory among the boulders, which made me think of Dutch: was he hanging back to protect the access to the ladder?

I straightened up to look around, finning slowly to keep from touching the coral. I located the anchor line and then the staghorn coral. I was searching for a line of exhaled air bubbles when Dutch came up behind me, still swimming well off the bottom as if uncommitted to the search.

He pointed obliquely down toward a spot beyond the staghorn and gestured thumbs up. Then he kicked for the surface.

At this shallow depth I knew that I had hours of bottom time, but I checked my computer to make sure before I followed him up toward the bright surface.

When I broke through he was already hanging onto the

anchor line, mask on top of his head and grinning. I swam up alongside him and raised my mask.

"Buenas tarde Señor Galeón," he said, raising his right hand for a high five.

"You went right back to it?" I asked.

"No. Took me a few minutes. Damn thing's moved."

"Moved?"

"Now it's wedged in some coral, or rocks or something."

"How could a brass cannon move?"

He tossed an open-palm gesture. "I don't know – maybe somebody's been messing with it. Tried to get it up and lost it, y'know what I'm saying? Anyway, that's where it is and I think I know how we can bring it up. Come on back to the boat."

He released the anchor line and swam away. I followed, trying to sort out the implications of someone else working the site and thinking, here it comes – he's going to get in the boat and tell me how to go down and rig a sling. I decided to say I needed to blow a few minutes before I start back down. When I was in the boat we could negotiate. But when we got to the ladder he motioned for me to climb up. I worked off my fins, threw them into the cockpit and climbed aboard, leaving Dutch hanging on the bottom run of the boarding ladder.

With the mask on the top of his head he said, "There's a hank of dinghy line – eighth, maybe three-sixteenths inch – in the chain locker. Bring it out and we'll use it for a telegraph when I'm down there."

Trying to remember what Roger had said about rights to a treasure site – something about staying there to protect the claim – I carried my mask and fins, padding barefoot through the cabin into the forecastle, and opened the chain locker hatch. If someone had been trying to recover the cannon but had left the site, I decided, then it was probably ours if we could get it

167

up. I tossed my gear inside to keep it out of the way and separate from the tangle of gear in the cockpit. Then, already sweating in the airless space, I unbuckled my knife, stripped off my wet suit and piled them in too.

My swim trunks and tee shirt clung damply as I searched for the dinghy line, which turned out to be twisted in the suspenders of a cracked and torn pair of foul weather pants. I shook out the tangles as I dragged it back through the cabin, wondering how much it would take to bribe Dutch to stay on this site until Roger could get a boat up here. When I came back out into the cockpit, Dutch was still hanging onto the bottom rung of the ladder.

I tossed him an end of the dinghy line and he tied it to the D-ring on the left shoulder of his inflatable vest, saying, "Now uncleat the gin pole and pull off some slack. I'll swim both lines down and rig some kind of a sling on the gin pole line. Cannon's wedged tight as teen pussy and so we'll have to work it loose. When I jerk the telegraph once, you take a strain on the gin pole. When I jerk twice, give me some slack. When I get her loose and off the bottom I'll jerk three. That means I'm coming up to help you lift her. We'll need both of us on deck to take her aboard without bashing something."

He adjusted his tank harness as I started pulling slack off the gin pole. Leaning to haul the three-eights inch nylon through the pair of two-sheave blocks, I realized why it had been recently rigged with new line out of a big coil: Dutch had been trying to raise the cannon with it. He said, "Pay out both lines as I go down so I don't get tangled up in the slack, okay?"

"Okay," I said. "And when I give you a jerk, hold up. Means I have to pull some more slack off the gin pole. Two jerks means go ahead."

He nodded and said, "Pull three if you want me to come up.

Like, maybe you see a shark fin." He grinned to make that a joke and then said, "You see anything I could use like a crow bar? Damn thing's really wedged."

I glanced around the cockpit and then went through the cabin and the forecastle. When I came back to the top of the ladder he'd tied the gin pole line in a loose bowline to a D-ring on his right shoulder. I said, "Only thing I see is the gaff. I think that's too clumsy."

He nodded. "Too long. I couldn't handle it down there. I'll just use the dive knife." He spit in his mask and rinsed it out, stuffed in the mouthpiece, took a couple of breaths to check the flow, seated the mask, signaled thumbs up and pushed off, letting the belt take him down.

I took one line in each hand, holding both arms out to maintain separation and squeezing light pressure as they ran across my palms. As I watched the coils pay out I was trying to imagine who might have tried to lift the cannon and dropped it. Roger knew approximately where the site was. He could have hurried his sea trials and put a diver down, but he'd never leave a site up for grabs.

Twice I signaled a pause to pull more line through the blocks, and once to clear a kink before it jammed a sheave. After what seemed a long time, the lines stopped running through my hands and I sat on the gunwale, trying to keep a gentle belly of slack to give Dutch freedom to work.

One jerk. I gave an answering jerk and went to the gin pole. Keeping my foot on the telegraph line so that it didn't spill slack overboard, I uncleated the downhaul and pulled it taut. I picked up the telegraph line with my left hand and heaved on the downhaul with my right.

Two jerks. I slacked off the downhaul and waited, imagining Dutch levering a barnacle-crusted gunbarrel free with his dive knife. If this turned out to be a treasure site, then wouldn't I be entitled to a full share? At least one, surely.

Over the next twenty minutes or so I took a strain and slacked off half a dozen times. Then, when I felt one jerk and took a strain, the downhaul kept running through the blocks. I put my foot on it to hold the tension while I reached up for another heave. No resistance. The telegraph line jerked once again, and I took two long heaves on the downhaul. I imagined the cannon swinging free, perhaps eight feet off the bottom. I was about to bring it up another two or three feet when I felt three telegraph jerks.

I cleated the downhaul and began bringing in the telegraph line as fast as I could. There was so much slack that Dutch seemed to be bolting for the surface. Not a good idea, even at these shallow depths, but before I had half the telegraph line in the cockpit I saw him break water a few yards off the bow, raising both hands, thumbs up.

I brought in the line and heaped it under the transom as he swam to the ladder and then, as he took off his fins and tossed them aboard, I went back to the gin pole. The cannon was coming up so easily I felt no weight. "That's far enough," Dutch said from the top of the ladder. "I'll get a fender to help us bring her aboard."

"Doesn't feel like we'll need anything," I said as he went past me into the cabin. "You sure the cannon didn't slip off again?"

"Gin pole's rigged for heavyweight fish," he said from inside. "Don't worry – I watched it going up far enough to make sure."

I heard a door close, but I was looking at a white ball fender that had surfaced. Remembering that Dutch had tied it to the cannon with fifteen feet of line, I was trying to peer down into

the water below it so that, by the time I recognized the sound –
the hanging locker – and turned around, Dutch was standing in
the companionway with both dive knives in his hand. He tossed
mine overboard.

"You've been nosing around, haven't you Burke?" He held
the knife loosely in his right palm, pointing at my belly. "Why
don't you tell me where you put the shotgun shells? Make this
a lot easier for both of us."

I backed away, putting the swiveled fighting chair between
us. "Didn't think we'd need a shotgun to bring up an old
cannon," I said. "What's the problem, Dutch?"

"Problem is–" he put the knife in his teeth and grabbed the
downhaul, which was backing off slowly through the blocks,
and then, slurring around the blade in his mouth "–what we're
bringing up isn't just some old brass cannon I can let you have
for a couple of hundred bucks."

Keeping his clear blue eyes on me, he brought in line. I
glanced around the cockpit. His fins and mask were tumbled on
the heap of telegraph line under one corner of the transom, the
tangle of cast net and weighted belt under the other, the bait
knife was stuck in the port rod holder, just below Dutch's elbow
as he heaved on the down haul, and the five-foot gaff in the
starboard rod holder. As if he'd heard what I was thinking, he
glanced down at the bait knife and interrupted his down-
hauling long enough to grab it out of the holder and toss it
overboard.

"That's no problem," I said. "I was just looking for a practice
dive. This is your site."

He face changed into what I thought was a smile around the
knife. Alongside the floating fender a metal drum broke the
surface, trussed up to the gin pole line. Holding the line to keep
just the top of the drum out of the water, he took the knife out

of his mouth and waved it toward the stern. I stepped back into the starboard corner of the transom and said, "Whatever's in there, it's all yours." I realized now what it probably was, and how gullible I'd been.

He brought the cigarette laugh up from his chest. "Thank you, Burke. Nothing like looking at a sharp edge to bring out the generous side of a man, is there?" He put the knife back in his teeth and brought in the downhaul carefully until the drum was hanging just over the gunwale. Then, without cleating the line, he grabbed the drum and swung it inboard, letting the line back off through the blocks as the drum settled to the deck.

He dropped to his knees and, still keeping his eyes on me, began to slice the duct tape that sealed the top. "Ever see a million dollars, Burke? Maybe a million and a half, if I handle the marketing right. Hell of a lot more interesting than an old brass cannon, don't you think?"

"It's all yours," I said. "You can deal me out."

He laughed again. "Don't want to get involved in my commodity business? Don't worry." With most of the tape cut he used the knife to lever the top open as he said, "Don't worry your little head–" the top came off with a hollow, bongo sound and he leaned over, his face in the drum.

I crabbed along the gunwale, moving as quickly as I could without turning my back to him. He took out a small mushroom anchor shackled to a short length of chain. I grabbed the gaff out of the rod holder and swung it around toward him as he reached back into the drum.

As I jerked off the cork that protected the point, I was thinking that if I could get the gaff into his right shoulder he'd have to use the knife with his left hand, but at that moment he looked up at where he thought I should be, and then around to where I was, tipping the drum to let me see inside. "Would you look at that?" He seemed not even to notice the five-foot gaff with the hook end pointing toward him as he banged the handle of his knife against the drum and asked, "You see what she did?" Instead of lunging to sink the gaff in his shoulder I glanced into the empty drum.

He dived under the gaff to land on his right shoulder and rolled onto his feet in the knee of the stern, knife belt-high and ready. I took a step away, holding the gaff across my body, hands about eighteen inches apart, to use either the point or the butt. We circled the fighting chair.

Bright blue eyes locked into mine, left hand slightly forward like a tightrope walker's, Dutch orbited the knife around a point above the toe of his right dive bootee as he sidled counterclockwise around the chair. I was trying to remember what the marine sergeant had told us, back in the Academy, about watching a man's waist to anticipate his shoulder moves.

"Looks like we have a stand-off," I said as we completed the second circuit of the chair. He stopped, the chair between us. Trying for a let's-be-reasonable tone, I said, "Why don't we just agree that none of this happened?"

He thought about that. "You know, we almost could. No damage done, right? You've done me no dirt, and you're not the kind of guy I want to see floating around out here with your dick in your mouth."

I must have reacted, remembering what Scully had said about the way they found Armond, because Dutch laughed hoarsely and lowered the knife to his side. "Let's just cool it for a minute and think about that, okay?" He gestured with the knife and I took a step back, into the knee of the transom. Moving slowly, with the knife back up at the ready, he climbed into the fighting chair.

I leaned against the gunwale, keeping the gaff ready with the butt off the deck. Dutch pulled out the tail of his wet-suit shirt and, never taking his eyes off me, began to slice it open, working from his belly toward his chin. His body hair was black, in contrast with his blond head. "Need a little ventilation," he said with that ingratiating smile. "We've finished diving for today and you're out of your suit, so I think I'll get comfortable."

If he put the knife in his teeth to pull his arms out of the sleeves I was ready to sink the gaff in his right shoulder. But when he had the shirt open to his chin he dropped his knife hand to his lap, palm up with thumb and knife pointed toward me.

"You see," he said, "the problem we have here is–"

Some reaction more primitive than thought moved the gaff handle. By the time an image congealed in my mind, the knife had been deflected and Dutch was past, the momentum of his leap out of the chair carrying him into the gunwale. My awareness arrived too late to follow the parry with the butt of the gaff into the nape or the kidney. Instead, I stabbed after him, hooking the point into the space vacated by his twisting back as he rolled away on the gunwale like a prize fighter along the ropes and whipped around to face me again with the knife back in the ready position and a big smile on his face.

"Good move, Burke. How many more of those do you have?"

"As many as I need, Dutch." My voice wobbled a little, and I cleared my throat to lower and steady it. "But what do I need moves for?"

He nodded, still smiling. "It's nothing personal, Burke. You see, what I was saying, what we have here–" he raised the knife "–is offense against defense. I've just got this little blade against all the wood in that gaff handle. But when I move the blade–" he feinted a thrust and laughed hoarsely at my reaction

"–I take the action to you. Now that gaff – all that wood – you've got to stay around home and wait for me. It's just too heavy and clumsy to hook a guy like me. Nimble, you notice that?"

"Like I say, Dutch, this is a standoff. What we need is a deal."

Moving one careful step at a time he went back to the chair. He put his left hand on the left arm and shifted his weight, moving the knife point toward me. I took an involuntary step back and he was seated again, knife point orbiting again above his right toe.

"Okay," he said, "what are you offering?"

"Well, I know what's going on in the Armond investigation," I bluffed.

"Armond?"

"Dutch, we keep playing games, you won't learn a thing."

He glanced down at his knife hand, thinking about that. When he looked up his eyes were wide blue innocence. "How'd you learn about Armond up there in Jupiter? You know, where the diving was murky, day before yesterday."

I forced a smile. "All right, you got me there. But the letter of marque – I really do have a deal with Jolly Roger."

"From the date on that contract," he said, making it a statement.

"You don't forget, do you?"

"So let's both of us stop playing games and you let me see a sample of the goods. What could I learn from you?"

"You could learn what the cops are looking for. What kind of a suspect."

"That's interesting. Go on."

Playing for time, I said, "He have something to do with that drum we pulled up? What was supposed to be in it?"

Dutch tossed the knife into his left palm and laughed as I jerked the gaff down across my belly. "See what I mean, Burke? Offense calls the tune. You just have to stay ready all the time, but I can pick my moment." He tossed the knife back into his right hand. "Okay, why not? Sure, Armond was our connection."

"So why did he wind up…" I hesitated.

"Floating in his pool with his dick in his mouth? Because he held out on me. Like you, Burke."

"Held out on you? I'm out here helping you find what you're looking for, remember?"

"You're holding out the shotgun shells on me." He tilted the blade and ran his thumb along the edge. "End of the day, that won't do you any more good than it did sweet Armond. Unless, like you say, we can make a deal. So what do you know about the police investigation?"

"What do I get?" I asked. "If I tell you, what does it buy me?"

"Good will. Make me feel like we can trust each other. Trust is important, don't you think?"

Sweat tickled a path down my back. It occurred to me that I hadn't finished *The Great Gatsby*. Hadn't taken Gregg bone fishing. Come to think, hadn't taken Marge bone fishing. Lot of things I still wanted to do. Trying to establish a conversation, I played back his language: "Sure, trust is important. We need to feel like we can trust each other."

I realized that I'd let the butt of the gaff settle to the deck and lifted it again into the ready position. Could I move fast enough to get behind the chair before he could out of it? Not now, when he was tossing the knife from hand to hand. Keep the conversation going and look for a distraction. I asked, "Ever hear of homophobic rage?"

He rasped a chuckle. "Cop-talk for whacking a queer. It was

the dick in the mouth that gave 'em that idea, right?"

"Probably a clue," I said.

He heard the irony and nodded, still smiling as if enjoying a private joke. "Actually, he did – it wasn't about that. What it was about, was the money, really. I told him we'd had to ditch the goods and it was taking more time to bring them up than we'd figured – so we needed a little advance."

We'd had to ditch the goods. *We* needed a little advance. A memory connection closed. There was no tank in the forecastle. He said he'd stowed Joey's tank out of sight forward, in case Gisu was watching with binoculars as he came in. Without thinking it through, just trying to create some psychological advantage, I took a shot: "Did Dutch hold out on you too?"

He flashed that white smile and pointed a "you got it" finger at me. "I was wondering how long it was going to take you. Actually, Dutch played everything straight up with me, just about like I told you."

"Who shared whose air?"

"Dutch was a lot better diver than I am."

"But in spite of that…"

He shrugged. "I didn't have any choice. Dutch's problem was information."

I prompted: "He was with you when you found it."

"Actually, he found it. I should have let him help me bring it up – he didn't tell me it was wedged into the coral down there. I was in too big a hurry to get back into the boat."

I realized I'd let the butt of the gaff settle to the deck again and lifted it back into position. "Getting heavy?" he asked.

"You were in a hurry to get back to the shotgun."

He smiled and shrugged a little "whatever" gesture. I asked, "How'd you know Dutch had a gun on board?"

He looked down at the knife in his right hand, raising it off his lap as if testing its weight and balance. "Actually, he told me. When we were chasing that boat off the dive site. I asked Dutch, what are we going to do if we catch up? And he said we could rattle some number fours off the hull, just to make sure they get the message. He didn't tell me where he kept it, but it wasn't hard to find. Wasn't hard for you to find either, was it?"

"That was a nice little boat you torched," I said.

"Belonged to somebody in Miami, but his ex uses it." He pointed at me with his left hand. "Now I get it. You must have been using it too. Is she the unfinished Key West business?"

"What about *your* Key West business?" I asked. "Without Armond, what were you going to do with that can full of coke?"

"Pure Colombian? Dozen places I could move that. Most dealers can't take that much all at once, of course"

"Armond could?"

"He had off-shore accounts. Said he could raise a million and a half in two trips to the bank."

"But he wouldn't give you an advance?"

The pleasant, conversational smile disappeared and he spat the answer: "Fag. Couldn't pass up a chance to score."

"He came onto you?"

Just as quickly as they had disappeared, the smile and composure were back. "Said the commodity business is cash and carry. That probably would have been the end of it. I was pissed, but I probably would have just – shit, I understand cash and carry. But then he said if I need some walking around money, there're plenty of opportunities in Key West for a nice dresser with a pretty moustache. And, of course, he could show me how to make the best of my chances. Starting right then and there – four o'clock in morning on the edge of his pool. I was pissed anyway, but when he zipped down his fly, well, that did it."

"You popped him with the statue?"

He smiled and nodded, as if remembering a joke. "Had a dong out of Armond's dream, that statue did. It was just standing there in the hibiscus with its handle out, waiting. So, where're the cops looking for their homophobic hot head?"

To keep this going, I asked, "what happened to your moustache?"

He raised one finger to his upper lip. "Sometimes I miss it. But Joey had to go. It was easy. Shave the moustache, drop the fake doubloon overboard and leave the cravats aboard *Happy Daze*. That's all there ever was to Joey. All anyone will remember."

Playing back his language again, I said, "The doubloon was fake?"

"Bought it in Curacao. Tourists shop called 'Fools' Gold.' Looked real, didn't it? Anyway, it was easy to morph into Dutch." And then, mimicking himself mimicking Dutch, "Y'know what I'm saying? Just to be sure, I peroxided the hair and eyebrows too."

He flapped the sliced-open shirt to move some air across his belly. "Of course, now that you know about Armond and Dutch you've got an information problem too. Curiosity killed the treasure hunter, Burke. Nothing personal."

"Makes it easier to take," I said.

He chuckled. "Glad you understand. Now, the only thing left to negotiate is whether it's going to be quick and easy with the shotgun, or slow and miserable with the knife."

"Was there ever anything else to negotiate?"

Still wearing the friendly smile he shook his head. "Not really." He gestured toward the opened drum on the cockpit deck behind him. "Once you knew about that, smart guy like you, Burke, you were going to put the rest of it together. Enough of it, anyway. Now I think you're going to be smart enough to understand what the deal is."

"So what's the deal?"

"The deal is, we don't have much of a moon tonight. Not quite a new moon, but it's just a little more than a sliver." He moved slowly forward in the chair, watching my eyes, and then stood, moved around the gimbaled rod socket and backed toward the companionway. I glanced at the clutter in the cockpit. The leaded belt might give me some protection from the knife, if I could move it fast enough. Out of the water, it was heavy. Dutch – I was still thinking of him as Dutch – reached behind into the galley, rucked around blindly on the shelf until he came out with a pack of Camels and a book of paper matches.

"Don't get it yet?" he said, shaking a cigarette far enough out to get it in his mouth and pull it the rest of the way from the pack. "You see, the deal is," he doubled a match over and thumbed it alight, "it'll be a dark night." He lit the cigarette and exhaled two streams from his nose as he reached back to return the pack and matches to the galley shelf. "Couple of hours, the sun will go down. Maybe less. Then, hour or two after that, it's going to be black out here." He patted his chest. "Black as my heart. Now do you get it?"

"Advantage offense," I said.

"You get it." He came back to the chair, shifting the knife again into his right hand. "You and I, we'll just be shadows. You won't even be able to see the knife. That big old gaff is already getting heavy to hold up there at parade rest, isn't it?"

One careful step at a time, he moved around to stand in front of the chair. "Some time tonight, in the dark–" he feinted a thrust and laughed when I waggled the gaff handle. "So why put yourself through all that, just to wind up gutted like a grouper?"

Grouper. "Is that what she was looking for?"

He sat down and waited for me to go on.

"Gisu," I said. "She was always walking the beach at low tide. Was she looking for a square grouper?" I gestured toward the drum with the hook of my gaff. "For that?"

He pursed his lips, thinking about what I'd said. "She walked the beach?" he repeated.

"At low tide. I thought she was looking for something out at sea."

"Walked the beach at low tide," he repeated. "What'd you say she was looking for? Grouper?"

"Square grouper. Mary Jane. Bales tossed overboard when the Coasties show up. She was looking for something a whole lot more pricey, wasn't she?"

He pulled a hit on the Camel and then shook his head, exhaling streams of eddying smoke. "Stupid broad. She believed what I said about the trade winds. Was she out there every day?"

"I don't know. I only saw her twice." The moment was drifting off, detached from reality. We were acquaintances. Friends, even, sharing the solution of a puzzle. Something abstract, theoretical. If I could just keep building this relationship of mutual discovery, surely I could find some basis for negotiation. At the same time, I knew better. I knew about combat denial, the narcotic of tension fatigue.

"But it was low tide, both times?" he said.

"Both times. She said it was her zen, walking the beach."

"Low tide," he repeated, nodding as if listening to an explanation in his head. "Of course – she never took it out of the dink. If I hadn't been so high on the merchandise – when did you see her last?"

I tried to get back into the moment. What was the right

answer, now that I had something he wants? "Matter of fact," I said, "she was trying to hire me."

He pointed with the knife. "Hire you?" And then, comprehension blooming into a broad smile: "Oh. To take care of me, right?" He shook his head slowly, marveling. "Isn't she beautiful? Well, here's your chance."

"If I'd signed on, Dutch – Joey–"

"Dutch. Today I'm Dutch." He tossed a left-handed gesture. "Who do you want to be?"

I ignored that to press my argument: "If I'd signed onto her deal, you wouldn't *have* a next week. You'd be in the water now. I'd have cut the anchor and taken off."

He flipped the cigarette butt casually over the gunwale and unsnapped the flap pocket on the right sleeve of his wet suit. Fumbling a moment, he extracted a ring of three keys. "Unless you know how to hot wire a diesel, you weren't going to get very far without me." He dangled the keys teasingly and then, eyes not leaving mine, he tried to stuff them back into the pocket. The wet stretch-fabric stuck together. He glanced at the pocket once, momentarily, and I readied the gaff. "But what I counted on was, your eyes got squinty when I talked about treasure. Same way Gisu's do when she sees a blackjack table." He gave up trying to pry his pocket open and stood up again.

"I never considered it, Dutch. You know, what she wanted – I never considered leaving you out here."

"So you want me to feel like I owe you for that?" he said, backing around the chair again toward the companionway.

"You're pissed at her, I understand that. But you and I – we don't have any beef."

He shifted the keys to his knife hand and mopped his left palm across his mouth and down his throat, which was glistening in the sun. "This damn suit's turning me into a dim sum. You're right, Burke, I don't have any beef with you." He raked the wet blond hair off his forehead. He shifted the knife to his left hand and, keeping his eyes on me, reached through the companionway to drop the keys on the galley shelf with the cigarettes. "I'll bet there's somebody back home, where ever that is – you have a wife, Burke?"

"Ex wife. But I have a son."

"A son." He nodded, as if he'd expected something like that, and sat on the gunwale next to the gin pole, which left a safe distance between us. "I'll bet there're things you'd like to talk to your son about."

I lowered the butt of the gaff to the deck, easing the tension in my shoulders. "Yes, there are."

"Maybe, about treasure hunting?"

"In a way, I suppose so." I wondered where this was going.

"In what way?"

Reality seemed to be drifting off again. I heard myself answering as if to someone genuinely interested in me: "Well, I'd like to talk to him about not getting so caught up in what he's doing so he doesn't pay attention to what he's becoming."

He cocked his head, thinking about that. "Anybody else who's – unfinished business for you?"

I hesitated, and then answered the simple truth: "Yes, I have some unfinished business in Key West."

"Tell you what." He leaned forward, elbows on knees and arms crossed so that the knife pointed outboard, guileless blue eyes wide. "I'll let you get back into your wet suit and blow up the vest. That'll keep you afloat until a shrimper or a fisherman comes along and picks you up. Give me time to get on up the coast, and you can get back to Key West and take care of business."

I tried to keep a poker face as I considered that. The idea was seductive, even though I knew it was suicidal. What if I rushed him now, while he was sitting on the gunwale with the knife in his lap, making sweet and reasonable? In my mind's eye I saw him fumbling for the knife and then standing just as I lunged the curve of the gaff into his belly, shoving him back against the gunwale and then overboard. But his feet were apart on the deck, up on balls and toes, ready to move. If he slapped the thrust of the gaff away he'd be inside with the knife. I decided to keep the conversation going. "I don't know, Dutch. I haven't seen any boats out here all afternoon."

He glanced around. "You just haven't been noticing," he said. "Treasure on your mind. There're always boats going by, on the way to Big Pine, one of the other keys."

I scanned the empty horizon, trying to remember the chart on the wall of Roger's office. There wouldn't be any shrimpers in forty or fifty feet of water around a forest of coral heads, I knew that. And this time of year the sport fishing was in the bays and harbors for tarpon, back on the flats for bonefish and permit, and on the edge of the Gulf Stream for jacks and mahi mahi. One of those off-shore fishermen might troll past here. Maybe, in a week or two.

I remembered returning from missions, how tiny the carrier looked in the immensity of ocean, and imagined floating out here alone in the dark, maybe watching the lights of a cruise ship on the horizon. "Any flares on this boat?" I asked.

He nodded. "You're right – sometimes it's hard to see a man in the water. Let me think. Sure – I know where they are. Three flares. They're up on the bridge. I'll get them while you're putting on your suit."

If there were any flares aboard, I didn't think they'd be up on the bridge. Probably somewhere in the cabin, with the tools and spare parts.

"My wet suit's clear up in the chain locker. I put it up there to get it out of the way."

He rubbed his left knuckles against the grain of his two-day bristles, thinking about that. "I guess you don't want to put that gaff down and get on your hands and knees to get it out, right?"

"How about if you bring it out to me?"

He smiled and nodded, as if discussing reasonable alternatives. "Have a better idea. I'll stand over there in the stern sheets and you go into the cabin. Go in backwards, okay? Keeping your gaff up and ready. And then I'll drop the hatch boards in. After that, the only way for me to–" he opened his left palm as if to show he was hiding nothing "–you know, bother you, I'd have to lift the boards out, and you'd hear them scrape. Plenty of time to drop what you were doing." He mopped his throat again. "Not that I'm going to bother you. Not now, when you understand what the deal is."

I bit my lip to keep from reacting too quickly. I nodded slowly, thinking about the box of shells I'd stuffed into the toe of the rubber boot. In two steps I could grab the shotgun – surely he hadn't had time to find the key and turn the lock on the hanging locker door – and then I could dive into the forecastle. Even if he was pulling out the hatch boards I'd have time to fish out the shells, break the shotgun, drop two into the chambers and "–Okay," I said, "that sounds reasonable."

He sat forward in the chair and I jerked the gaff handle into position. "So that's where they are," he said. "Somewhere in the cabin. I figured if you didn't drop the shotgun overboard, you probably didn't drop the shells over either. But I couldn't be sure."

CHAPTER 11
The Whole Deal

"So you know they're inside somewhere," I said. "So what?"

"Just closing off your last option. When it starts to get dark, you could go up on the foredeck with the gaff and wedge yourself in front of the bowsprit. Narrow as it is up there, I'd have trouble getting past that gaff in the dark."

He tossed the knife into his left hand and then back to his right without dropping the bright blue gaze. "All you'd have to do is stay awake. But now that I know the shells are aboard somewhere, I could just–" he gestured over his shoulder toward the companionway "–pick up the keys, go below and take my time until I find them." He raised his elbows to create space. "In close quarters a five foot gaff isn't much good, is it? But just to be sure, I could drop the hatch boards in."

"You've got it figured out," I said, trying to keep the conversation going in the hope that something would surface that I could use. "I still don't really understand the deal. Like, what was it Gisu took out of the dink?"

He grinned and shook his head as if amused at his own folly. "Nothing. That's the point. She left it in there. She was supposed to be packing it into the drinking water can. You know, water in the tanks was Haitian, which is okay for showers, but I wouldn't put it in my mouth. Anyway," he gestured over his shoulder with the knife, "I was up there running the boat, where I couldn't see what she was doing in the cabin. Knowing her, I should have checked before she had the drum taped shut." He waved a little "you know" gesture. "But we'd been into the merchandise and I was all lit up."

"You were out bound from Haiti?"

He glanced at the sun, obviously estimating how much daylight remained. "You want to know the whole deal, don't you? Okay, what'd she tell *you*?"

He brought the knife back into the ready position, stood and walked back to the chair. Maybe, if I could keep this going … "That she was your sex slave," I said.

He laughed, nodding recognition. "From Thailand, right? Gisu, the sex queen of Siam."

"Next door. Best little whorehouse in Ho Chi Minh City."

"That's a new one," he said, sliding back into the seat with the blade up and ready. "Gisu – if that really is her name – she's the daughter of a dentist in Oak Park. Anyway, that's what she told me."

"Matter of fact," I said, "I noticed her teeth."

"She started going to the casino boat in Joliet when she was in high school. Met a guy who took her to Vegas. Been going to casinos and meeting guys ever since."

"Met you in Haiti?"

"No, I told you – she picked me up in Curacao. Haiti, that's our bargain basement."

"For coke?"

He nodded. "Place called Gonaïves."

"Never heard of that. I've been to Port au Prince, but I never heard of – what's the name?"

"You wouldn't. Kind of a drop zone for Colombian merchandise. No cop for miles. The locals are living like, well, they don't have anything to lose, you know? And so sometimes they mob the planes on the landing strip."

"Mob the – the planes don't have any protection?"

He raised those thick blond brows in a "you must be kidding" expression. "Usually a guy standing on the wing with an AK-47, what I'm told. But the Haitians run right at him. Like I say, they've got nothing to lose. If enough of them keep coming, sometimes they get their hands on the nose candy. Then they'll sell it cheap. Bargain basement."

"And you bring it up here to sink it off Key West?"

Casually, he scratched his neck with the point of the knife. "Not the first couple of times. Pretty little American sport fish with two pretty little Americans – spiffy silk scarf and black moustache – we just loafed along with the trade wind at our backs and nobody bothered us. When we got to Key West we tied up to the mooring and negotiated the sale with Armond and then headed north. Simple. But this time, somebody – I don't know what went wrong. Whatever, couple hundred miles out, the Coasties had a plane over us. We knew that before we got into Key West there'd be a cutter alongside. And a search."

"So you put it in the water can and sank it," I filled in, "figuring you'd come back and bring it up. What went wrong – you write down the wrong GPS numbers?"

He shook his head. "No. I was buzzed, but not that far gone. Mistake I made was reading the depth finder. I thought we were in eighteen, twenty feet of water. Must have been reading one of those coral heads. And I didn't realize how broken the bottom was. What I think is, we probably dropped the can on a coral head and it slid off, down into that gully or whatever you call it."

"But you finally found it."

"Yesterday." He rubbed his chin and flicked his forefinger against the memory of Joey's moustache. "But I couldn't raise it. Not by myself. You know, the way it was wedged in there. So what else can you tell me about the Armond investigation?"

"Only what the cops say they found at the scene."

"Which is?"

189

"First, I still don't understand about the dink."

He glanced at the sun again and mopped his face and neck. "You know, Burke, you're beginning to be a pain in the ass. Hour or two and it's going to be dark. Why don't you make it easy for both of us?"

Still trying to find some crack of negotiating room, I said, "If you were me, wouldn't you want to understand the deal before you made it easy?"

He arched the peroxide brows and nodded. "All right. Sure – why not?" He started to cross his legs but thought better of it. "Here's the picture. I'm on the bridge in a happy daze – I've wondered if maybe that's what caught the Coastie's attention, the cute name Gisu gave the boat – anyway, we're on our way to Key West where sweet Armond can come up with a million, million and a half with just a couple of trips to the bank. Not making real heavy weather, but four or five foot seas." He pointed the knife up. "Chopper's overhead. First it was some kind of a patrol plane."

"Four tails?" I prompted.

"I don't know – maybe. Anyway, he'd handed us off to the chopper. Next we're going to get the cutter, that's obvious. The goods are in the dink. Under the floorboards. Gisu and I, we decide the thing to do is to ditch – you know all that."

"Water drum, fifteen feet of line and ball fender," I filled in. "But instead, she puts in the dinghy anchor."

"I knew what she's like," he said, shaking his head. "Always looking for the main chance. But I was busy trying to keep those seas from breaking over the stern and watching the depth finder for a good spot to ditch. And I was buzzed." He looked around. "Breeze is freshening."

Now.

I aimed for the hollow between collarbone and neck but he

was already coming out the chair in a crouch, thumb along the blade and left forearm raised to deflect the gaff. I managed to interrupt the arc of the hook and step back on my left foot, shoving my right hand forward to swipe the butt of the gaff at his knife. He was waiting for me to commit the hook before he thrust and so he easily pulled away. As the gaff handle went past he feinted a lunge, forcing me another step back against the gunwale.

"Just wanted you to know I'm paying attention," he said. After a heavy-breathing moment, he reached behind with his left hand and located the fighting chair. "And I've got all the offense. Even in broad daylight." Not taking those smiling blue eyes off mine, he eased back into the seat. "Now let's see, where was I?"

"You were–" I had to clear my throat to steady my voice "– you and Gisu had decided to ditch the merchandise, only somehow it got replaced with a dinghy anchor."

"We were both cocky – full of chemistry – so Gisu must have decided to seal up the dinghy anchor in that drum and leave the coke under the floorboards. Then after dark, when the chopper couldn't see what we were doing, we put the drum overboard, she said–" I shot a quick look around the cockpit again: fins and mask on the telegraph line in one corner, weighted belt and cast net in the other, as he went on "–by that time we were coming down out of the happy daze, and I remember what she said. She said we hadn't been too careful re-sealing the plastic bag that we'd opened for our own stash, and maybe some of the coke got onto the dinghy."

Cast net.

I remembered the Tuscan frieze. Gladiator with trident and net.

Dutch went on: "I told her to scrub the dink down, but she

said she'd never get in all the seams of the rubber, not in the dark, and maybe we ought to just set it adrift and pick up a new one in Key West."

"So that's what she was looking for," I said, moving half a step to the right. "Every day at low tide, she was waiting for her ship to come in. Her dinghy."

He glanced around. The sun was red, sinking toward the horizon. "After all those lazy days, cruising along with the trade wind at our backs, Gisu must have figured that all she had to do was set the dink adrift and then wait for the wind to bring it home. Far fetched, but Gisu's a gambler. She acts like the odds don't apply to her. Besides, like I say, when she was supposed to be loading the water drum we were both flying high, up there where anything seems reasonable."

"I wonder what happened to the dinghy?" Another half step.

He shrugged. "Probably sank, eventually. That squall could have taken it way off shore. Somewhere there's a bunch of fish with a million dollar smile on their faces. But just in case, I'll be checking casinos until I find our Gisu."

"I guess she figured you would." Another. Out of the corner of my eye I could see the net within reach. "That's why she made me a proposition."

"She knew I'd be coming after her. Just like you know what's going to happen when it gets dark. Unless, now that you know the whole deal, you decide to make it easy on yourself."

"I've been thinking about that," I said, choking up on the gaff handle to put my left hand on the balance point. "What I think, Dutch, is–" I stooped quickly and grabbed a handful of the net "–I need an offense." The buckle of the leaded belt hung in the webbing but I was able to shake it free.

He was out of the chair, knife point orbiting again. "What you need, Burke–" he feinted with the knife and then tossed it into his left hand and, moving away from the gaff that was shortened up in my left hand, stepped in and sliced at my right side. I caught the blade on my right forearm and lashed the net like a whip. It wrapped once around his left wrist but he jerked loose, staggering back toward the companionway.

I moved to put the chair between us and used both hands to shake out the net, scattering blood from the gash on my right arm. Dutch was back in a crouch, tossing the knife from right and to left and back again as he moved away from the companionway counter clockwise, toward my gaff side and away from the net. I let go of the net with my left hand and lowered the point of the gaff to eye level. "This is the gladiator offense, Dutch. Evens things up. Now you want to talk about an arrangement?"

"You're no gladiator, Burke. Go ahead. Take your shot."

I feinted a pass at his face with the hook to move him back. "You don't want to work something out?" I said, blood running down the back of my hand to patter on the deck.

"What have you got to offer?"

"Well, how about—" I dropped the gaff and grabbed the rim of the net with both hands. I expected him to move back as I spun the net up and out, as high and as far as I could, but instead he jumped forward to plant his left foot on the gaff handle. The net bunched awkwardly in the air and most of it sailed past him, but the trailing edge hung under his left elbow. When he moved his arm he jerked the back of the net down around his head and shoulders, leaving his knife hand free under the leaded rim.

I backed away. "I didn't think you could cast it with one hand, Burke," he said, bunching the net in his left hand as he kept the knife ready in his right. "So now I've got 'em all. Offense *and* defense." Taking his time, he began collecting the net in his hand to lift it off his head and shoulders in one motion, keeping his foot on the gaff.

I looked around and grabbed the leaded belt by the buckle strap. As I started for him, Dutch raised his left arm, tangled in the net, and put the knife hand behind him. The belt made a *whoosh* as I brought it around with both arms extended and blood spraying. But before it hit his left knee Dutch dodged away, releasing the gaff.

The momentum of the weighted belt carried me two steps toward the stern. When I faced back around Dutch was against the gunwale lifting the net over his head. I looked at the gaff and then, without conscious thought, slung the diving belt.

He was leaning back to get his head free when the belt hit him in the chest. I grabbed the gaff. When I looked up, his feet in the wet booties were skidding off the deck as his back arched. Knife hand windmilling for balance, his head kept going down and the belt slid under his chin. He tipped back, farther, farther, and then dropped out of sight. One knee clung to the gunwale a moment. As the lead-rimmed net rattled over, he blurted a hoarse monosyllable just before he splashed in.

I don't know how long I stood there, staring at the gunwale. My arm was throbbing but I thought it was bleeding less. Then I heard him gasping, "Burke," and I went across the cockpit to look overboard. He was thrashing alongside. When he tried to say something he went under, and came up again. "Please – you can't – don't let me–" The dive belt buckle was tangled in the net, pulling him down.

I hesitated, and then, thinking that if I could get him up to the hull of the boat he could hang on while I went below and loaded the shotgun, I held the gaff down to him. Once I had the shotgun I could put the ladder over the side, let him climb aboard and make him take us back to Key West. He reached for the gaff with his free hand, but he was still holding the knife and he couldn't grab it. He went under again, longer this time.

He came up farther away, coughing and retching sea water. "Take it easy, Dutch," I called, remembering what he'd said about no time for calm analysis when you can't get your breath. "Just kick your feet. They'll keep you up."

"Net," he gasped. "Feet – net."

"Okay. Let go of the knife and grab this."

Still holding the knife he thrashed the surface, but now he was too far away even when I leaned out full length. When he went under again I jerked the life ring off the stern rack and waited, hoping that, weak and light-headed as I felt, I could pitch it accurately. But he didn't surface. After perhaps a minute I thought I saw bubbles. I considered diving for him, turning the idea around like an abstract proposition, but eventually decided that even if I could find the strength to deal with a powerful, panicky man, I had no business in the water with Dutch and a knife.

I sat on the gunwale, life ring in my lap, waiting for my heart and breathing to settle down and for the trembling to leave my knees. Fifty yards off the beam, ballyhoo leaped, skipped and leaped again to escape some menace below the placid, breeze-riffled surface. Finally, I began to think about what I was going to do now.

I could take the boat back to Big Pine – first, where were the keys? I remembered Dutch taunting me with them and then tossing them onto the galley shelf. I pushed myself upright, found that my knees didn't buckle and walked over to lean through the companionway. There, next to half a pack of Camels, were the keys.

I left them there as I looked around for a first aid kit, finally settling for a roll of black friction tape from the drawer under the settee and one of the clean white shirts in the hanging locker. Concentrating on each step as if this moment might dissolve into unreality, I found a galley knife, cut slits into the shirt tail and then, using my teeth and left hand, tore off two wide strips. The gash was only oozing now. I wrapped my arm as tightly as I could and taped the bandage in place.

Then I picked up the keys, climbed to the bridge, started the engine and took my time getting under way in the gathering dark. I circled the ball until the anchor came free and then, idling in neutral, I hauled it in, flaking the line down in careful figure-eights and stowing all the ground tackle in the chain locker as if I might need to use it again. As I worked I tried to think through my options.

Big Pine would soon be shut down for the night. I could tie up, row ashore and leave the dinghy at the dock, drive back to Key West and tell Roger I hadn't seen any sign of *Dutch Treat*. Eventually, probably as soon as another mooring fee was due, people would start looking for Dutch.

I replayed the day in my mind, trying to remember everyone who might remember me: bony kid with the tattoos at Stock Island who hadn't seen *Dutch Treat*, miss boobs and the jockey shorts guy at the Big Pine marina, sales clerk at Eckerd – if I couldn't remember her face, she almost certainly couldn't remember mine, nor could the waiter at the Sea Shanty.

But what if the word got back to Roger that *Dutch Treat* was abandoned in Big Pine harbor? I'd told him about Gisu's proposition and he'd put his thick finger on Big Pine as the most likely place to look for *Treat*. "You're not going up there because your pissed off about your friend's boat, are you?" he'd said. I imagined sitting across that steel and chrome desk, trying to explain to that little guy who occupied so much space how I could have failed to spot the boat in Big Pine harbor. Impossible. Okay, so *Dutch Treat* had to disappear tonight.

The dinghy was back on the mooring, and so whatever I did had to start within swimming distance. I checked the compass and looked east: no moonrise yet. Incongruously, I remembered Marge asking, "Why do they call it nightfall, when it gets dark from the ground up?" which intruded the question, what would I tell Marge? I put that aside for the moment, thinking about moonlight, and then I remembered that Dutch had said we wouldn't have much of a moon tonight. On a dark night, with no running lights I could slide *Treat* quietly into the mouth of the harbor after everything was closed up for the night, turn her around onto a course for whatever landfall is next – the Canary Islands, maybe – tie down the helm, slip her into gear and swim ashore. Dutch said he'd topped off the tanks before he left Key West, and so she'd mumble along on those reliable diesels until a tropical storm somewhere swamped her, along with the last artifacts of Joey Doubles, Dutch and the fools' gold.

I found the chart under the console and set a course for Big Pine. Who else had I talked to? Gregg, but I hadn't told him anything. I'd been planning to talk to him about transitions, and facing issues when they come up, how the longer you put off any part of growing up, the harder it is to get it done.

Harry, but I hadn't told him much. If I told him now, I could imagine what Harry would say: "This guy has been waiting all afternoon to gut you like a grouper, and then, when you get a lucky shot, you try to help him back aboard? How long had you been sitting in the sun without your hat?"

"He was terrified, Harry, and begging for help."

"Don't you suppose those little guys carrying their own rice were terrified too?"

"We couldn't see their eyes. Everything's gotten more complicated since then."

"It's always been complicated. You and I – we made it simple. Just put the ordnance on the target and the wheels back on the deck."

"We just made it *seem* simple, Harry. The real stuff was always in the complications."

"What real stuff?"

"Well, Marge, for one."

So what was I going to tell her? I thought about that night when we'd made pasta putenesca and talked about our failed marriages. I'd said I wasn't as generous as she was but I did take some of the responsibility for my divorce and she said, "In my book, responsible trumps generous every time." How was I going to explain turning the *Treat* loose and sneaking out of Big Pine?

Explaining self defense to Morales wouldn't be easy, but it would be easier than that. I pulled the chart out again and changed the heading toward Key West. Then, before I had time to talk myself out of it, I raised the marine operator on the ship to shore radio and asked her to patch through an emergency call to Detective Morales in Key West. I got Officer Somebody, who said Morales was off duty and connected me to his voice mail.

"I'll be in your office a ten tomorrow morning," I said, speaking slowly against the wind across the flying bridge. "I have a long story to tell your tape recorder, on one condition: I insist on a lie detector test."

CHAPTER 12
Ship Came In

Harry, Marge and I argued through most of a muggy night on his terrace about how to position Margaret's Two for the upscale resident market without losing the existing Margaret's clientele. At one point I told Harry, "For a silent partner, you're getting damned vocal" and he said, "For the smallest investor, you're talking damned tall." We finally decided that instead of a grand opening we'd throw a small party for what Marge called "our special friends," which meant genuine conchs who don't set foot on Duval between Halloween and Memorial Day.

The menu was Marge's, and not open for discussion. It began with a choice of conch chowder or a terrine of garden vegetables. After that came either hearts of palm vinaigrette or avocado with grapefruit sections. The entree was either grilled local lobster with black bean and corn salsa or medallions of pork with wild mushrooms on grilled polenta. Dessert was molten chocolate cake with vanilla crème Anglaise, or key lime pie. As guests arrived the waitresses passed orange blossoms and champagne, but the bar was open for serious drinkers, and during dinner we offered a Chiraz and a Bordeaux blanc.

On the night of the party Harry showed up early to help me set up the tables and accept the late deliveries while Marge was displaying temperament in the kitchen. We talked about Gregg, who was coming down for the spring tarpon run and maybe some bone fishing if the conditions were right, and the condo I'd rented on Grinnell. He didn't ask if Marge and I had any plans to consolidate households and I didn't volunteer that the subject was on my mind but not yet a matter of discussion.

By the time the dining room was in order, with a hibiscus

spray in a bud vase on every white linen table cloth, the bartender arrived. "This is our last chance for a beer," I said, "before haute cuisine begins. I've got an idea I want to try on you."

"I've got something for you too," he said, leading the way to place an inaugural foot on the brass rail. "You first."

"Once we get sales up to three hundred bucks a square foot with a fifteen percent margin," I said, "would you be ready to consider another venture?"

He jerked his elbow off the bar and made a theatrical grab for his wallet. "Let me guess: when the cops auction off *Dutch Treat* and *Happy Daze*, you want to buy them and start a sport fishing business."

I shook my head. "I don't want to see either one of those boats again. Or the cops." I tried to imitate Morales asking a statement: "Captain Bascomb, there's just a couple of points we'd like to go over again?"

"You out of the woods there?" Harry asked.

"They won't tell me that, but they haven't been around for the past couple of weeks to ask me the same set of questions for the forty-fourth time, or talk about another polygraph."

"Anything wash up that might be what's left of Joey Doubles?"

I shook my head. "And now they're treating *Dutch Treat* and *Happy Days* as abandoned property. Marge thinks they really want to believe my story. You know, close the Armond case, stop the heartburn it stirred up in conch society."

"So what's the venture. A treasure hunt?"

"No, something we know something about. Airplanes."

Marge blew through the swinging doors and waved, taking off her apron on the way to the ladies room to get ready for the first guests. "The local charter guy," I explained, "is fed up with the business, and Billy's customers are fed up with his attitude. Roger's diving two sites now, and he told me he'd sign a guaranteed minimum contract for pick up and delivery service he could depend on."

"How do you pick up people off a dive boat?"

"It's not a dive boat, it's a barge. And you don't pick up people, its computer tapes and bottom samples and little stuff like that. You rig a line and catch it with a tail hook, like old times. But Roger's just one customer. Cuba's got to open up pretty soon, you know that. We'd have the shortest hop from America to Havana. Of course, we'd have to stay clear of the narcotics trade and–"

"I'll think about it," Harry interrupted. He glanced around to make sure the bartender was out of earshot and took a tiny, brown-paper wrapped package from his pocket. "Now, before Marge comes out, here's something that came for you at my condo. Woman's handwriting, with no return address."

Making a show of having nothing to hide, I tore it open on the bar. Inside was a match box, smashed a little out of shape to house a white, two-dollar casino chip. Turning to get the light over my shoulder I could read, in raised letters, "Princess Beach Curacao NA."

"Somebody staking you to a game?" Harry asked.

"Wishing me luck, sort of. This is a lucky chip. Looks like, one way or another, her ship came in after all."

"And now she's giving away her luck?"

I finished my beer and turned around with my back against the bar to wait for Marge. "Luck is like love, Harry. First you have to give it away."

Also by Weyman Jones:

Books for Young Readers
The Talking Leaf
Edge of Two Worlds
Computer: the Mind Stretcher

Printed in the United States
1378800001B/448-459